The Race Against TIME

Solomon Ezonle Akossey

THE RACE AGAINST TIME
Copyright © 2023, Solomon Ezonle Akossey

E-mail: sakossey@gmail.com
Website: https://www.naseabooks.com
Telephone Number: 0240370479 / 0209538488
LinkedIn: shorturl.at/hkrsG

Book Cover designe by Ben Apaw
E-book digitising and layout designe by Sam K. Nyarko-Mensah

Ghana Library Cataloguing-in-Publication Data
Akossey, Solomon Ezonle
   The race against time / Solomon Ezonle Akossey. – Accra: Solomon
   Ezonle Akossey, 2023.
1. FICTION
I. Title
DDC 248 - - dc 21
ISBN: 978-9988-3-6789-3 (Paperback)   GLCN - 369
ISBN: 978-9988-3-6788-6 (e-book)   GLCN - 369
ISBN: 978-9988-3-6790-9 (Paperback, digital) GLCN - 369

to
Nana Serwah Danquah Afriyie.

1

Persevering through life's challenges can feel never-ending. Instead of simply waiting for difficult times to pass, it's about embracing them and finding a way to thrive even amidst adversity. The choices we make measure the wound or success of our future.

Decision-making has become a tug-of-war since sixteen sixty-six. Unfortunately, I came to realize that all choices rested in my hands. Although I've had friends by my side, their efforts to help me seemed futile. I knew I had the potential to succeed, but the challenge of making things work had been a constant source of frustration. Graduating from university with a first-class degree was my primary goal, but it remained elusive due to my consistent failure in meeting attendance requirements.

Life had been unjust to me; I've had to wander the streets in order to make ends meet. I traversed from car to car, shop to shop, and house to house, all in search of a day's meal, yet my efforts yielded no fruition. It was not an easy journey.

One hot afternoon, I spotted a gentleman from a distance across the street. He appeared handsome and charming, six feet tall and in a nice blue jeans' trousers. He walked towards me; as he mentioned my name, my heart went racing like an athlete completing a long-distance race.

"Sarah how are you doing?" he said softly with a smile.

"I'm doing well by His grace, not complaining," I replied, taken aback.

"Do you remember me?" he asked, winking at me.

His teeth showed beautifully white as he smiled, and his breath was very chill. I noticed he had come down from his air-conditioned car—a luxurious four-wheel drive sedan.

"No, I don't remember you," I lied, unfazed.

His good looks and smile did not steal my attention. My focus was on selling my belongings so I could afford to study for upcoming exams.

"Take this, my card. Please give me a call when you get home" he said, handing her his card.

"You're looking incredibly sweet, just like in the old days. I'm sure beauty is your hobby," he added, maintaining eye contact.

The card was elegantly simple, and I admired the colors and design. It seemed like everything about him was impeccable.

"I'll be waiting for your call, so please find time to reach out," he added before leaving for his car.

I looked away to avoid him noticing my gaze. My late mother had advised me about men, especially those with cars, who exploit women. They use sweet words to manipulate women and often lead them into compromising situations. Sometimes, the flashy car isn't even theirs.

With or without my parents' guidance, I had learned valuable lessons. I promised to remain chaste until the right man came along. I won't forget how Esi recounted her experience with a con artist who persuaded her that a carefree lifestyle meant achieving quick wealth by sacrificing her integrity.

During one of our annual talks for women empowerment, Esi's life story was quite touching. On stage, Esi was decently dressed in a blue long-sleeved shirt well tucked into her black pleated long skirt and a black flat shoe. As she held the microphone with so much confidence, she narrated…

In a time when society lacked respect for those who lacked direction, I was driven by curiosity to explore everything after I fell in love with a gentleman who happened to be a con artist. With him, smoking cigarettes was just the tip of the iceberg. He lured me into promiscuous living, dating all kinds of men for money. Whether they were tall, short, slim, or robust, I was open to them. Although I had my presentiments, his interest was much influenced by the money I received.

I was young, full of energy, and my complexion was an allure to men. Due to the dangers tied to my lifestyle, I resorted to spiritual practices and consumed various medicines without proper prescriptions. Even when I was menstruating, he talked me into getting medications from the pharmacy to stop my flow just to make myself available to men.

We were indeed successful. At my age, I had a ritzy apartment and a car, and one could say I literally had no needs. Eventually, he deceived me and gained possession of everything I had. I was so used to the glitzy life that I wasn't ready to relapse into a clean slate. Determined to get back on my feet, I was ready to go the extra mile in my promiscuous living.

Days and years went by until one night I had a peculiar, frightening dream. The sensation of God's presence touched me deeply, jolting me awake with a profound sense of guilt.

"Your body is the temple of God. If you don't care of it from this moment forward, I will take your life."

This voice echoed in my sleep that night. Driven by the urgency of the message, I sought deliverance from our pastor. Since then, I've been committed to educating the youth, especially young girls, about the dangers of seeking quick wealth.

Those words continued to reverberate in my mind as I sat on my bed. I recalled reading them in the Holy Bible. I, Esi, had faced a challenging period since that moment. Men who had previously dismissed me as a headstrong girl suddenly recognized my value. I had transformed but I carry the pain of no longer being a virgin. I pray to find genuine love one day – someone who will embrace me for who I am and not judge me based on my past.

"Given all this, do you think I should fall into this trap? I don't think I need to call…" Sarah mumbled upon looking at the card in her bag after that encounter.

"What's going on? Sarah hasn't called in the past three days" he said to himself confused.

"Did she lose the card, or are the details incorrect?" Raymond said as he retrieved a copy of the complimentary card he gave to Sarah to confirm the information on it.

Looking carefully at the information on the card, hc got positive.

"But the number is mine" he said that loud.

"The email address is active. My phone had been on, so what's happening?" he said again throwing his hands in the air as if to ask God why.

"I guess I need to go find her exactly where I saw her. I can't forget the radiance of her beauty over the years" Raymond said with smiles.

"I must hurry before she leaves the market square," he said softly to himself and started the car's engine.

Meanwhile, after an exhausting day, Sarah sought respite on a wooden bench near a grocery store. The surroundings were noisy, and the bench had tilted to the left, making it uncomfortable to rest. Her black jeans and sleeveless shirt gave her an unapproachable appearance. Hunger gnawed at her, and she needed money to cover her final semester's fees. Hope seemed distant as her thoughts grew fainter. She teetered on the brink of despair.

On that day, she had to sell all the sachets of water she had secured from the vendor, just to secure credit from the owner for the next day. Investing in education required money, she was struggling with finances for her school and so, engaging in menial jobs was her major means of survival.

I stood at crossroads, uncertain of my path. I wished I hadn't been born to face these adversities. The early loss of my parents had rendered me homeless. Both my family and church members had promised to support me, particularly in my education, during my parents' funeral.

"We will provide you with monthly support for your living expenses" the people at the funeral said to me.

"I'll grant Sarah a fifty percent scholarship once she's admitted to the university" another person at the funeral said to me.

"The church will aid you with all your needs. Just let us know, and we'll assign Elder Matthew and Deaconess Freda" the church pastor said, as he was preaching on that day of the funeral.

"There's a room available in my home. You're welcome to stay with my family whenever you decide" a church member hissed.

These assurances brimmed with sweet words, instilling hope, and security. Regrettably, they faded within a week, as everyone got rapt in their own affairs. The only funds I received from the funeral were used for my university admission, yet God, who promises and delivers on his word, remained my rock and refuge.

I don't hold my family and church members at fault; rather, I blame "death," which respects no one. What puzzled me most was Elder Matthew, who sought to exploit me.

"If you don't share my bed, I won't assist you with anything," his words pierced like a sword through me.

"It happened on a sunny afternoon as my parents were driving to a nearby town for an annual church conference. My father rode at a high speed, unaware that a sharp curve awaited him just two meters ahead" Sarah said and paused.

"At that moment, a call came from his close friend, prompting him to answer while still accelerating on the curve, deviating from his intended route" she added.

"We don't know where the other car came from; it collided with my parents' car, killing them instantly without a chance to utter a word," Sarah narrated, tears streaming down her face.

"I was incredibly fortunate because I chose to travel to the church conference on the bus organized by my church. I live because I was not with my mum and dad in their car. The exciting 'Jama' songs (popular gospel songs sung with hands clapping) from the youth and the humorous exchanges from others were enticing reasons. Richard's persistent talk about his interest in me was something I was unprepared for," she added, with tears welling in her eyes.

"Don't cry, Sarah. I'm here for you," a soft comforting voice intruded suddenly from behind.

She turned, only to come face-to-face with the same guy she had been intentionally avoiding for days.

"I don't need your help; and who says I'm crying?" she muttered, swiftly wiping away her tears.

"Don't pretend, dear. You spoke loudly, and I've been standing here for a while, hearing everything you've been saying about fees, hunger, and what struck me most was the sudden loss of your parents" he told Sarah looking straight into her eyes.

"As for the actions of your family and church members, I'd rather not delve into that" Raymond said in an angry tone.

"It's the same reason why I keep my distance from extended families and the church," he whispered, while holding her right hand.

By this time Sarah could not control or hide her tears; they flowed like rain drops. Raymond led her to his car; he drove to a popular boutique five metres away from where they stood to get her very expensive yet beautiful clothes and shoes.

They went to a restaurant afterwards to have lunch. The restaurant exudes an air of elegance and sophistication from the moment you step through its grand entrance. The exterior is adorned with tasteful architectural details, a blend of modern design and classic charm, inviting patrons to embark on a culinary journey like no other. The menu is a masterpiece, featuring a tantalizing array of culinary creations crafted by a team of skilled chefs.

After lunch, they went to settle her debt. Considering the situation then, Raymond saw the need to accommodate Sarah for as long as she wished.

"Forgive me for not introducing myself" he whispered softly.

"I am Raymond, and I work as the finance controller for SEA Group of Companies," he introduced himself with a broad smile as he drove.

"I already know your name and where you work. You gave me your card that day," Sarah responded, her smile matching his.

"I won't dwell on the reasons you haven't called me all this time" he said quickly upon seeing Sarah smile.

"What matters now is that you'll be staying at my place until you decide otherwise" he said as he drove towards his gate.

Sarah's face beamed with a surprise and a smile.

"Your fees will be taken care of, and any needs you have will be attended to," Raymond said with an assuring pride.

They pulled over at Raymond's house, and he stepped out of the car to open the door for her. After retrieving the bags of items they had purchased from the boutique from the back of the car, they made their way towards the door. Raymond reached into the pocket of his red shirt for the keys, unlocked the door, and ushered her inside, guiding her to a cozy couch. The apartment was spacious, boasting four bedrooms and adorned with luxurious decorations. As Raymond went to fetch drinks from the fridge, he reassured her that everything would be fine.

"Take this, have a drink, and don't be afraid. I see you as my sister, and you'll always be" Raymond confidently said.

"I've wanted to get closer to you, learn from you, and share whatever I have with you. So, please, feel at home; be free of fear and have a clear mind," he spoke as he sipped his drink.

That was the main reason I also took a drink. Anything can happen when a man wants something from you or wants to undermine your hard-earned accomplishments. The drink appeared clean and tasted good. That night, I was uneasy. I made sure to lock my door and kept the key with me. I even searched the room thoroughly to ensure there were no hidden cameras.

Truthfully, the place felt like home. It seemed Raymond had everything, prompting me to wonder if he was the caretaker or the landlord. I'm cautious around guys and always need to be a step ahead. They can be unpredictable.

Days, weeks, and months passed, but I never encountered any other woman in the house.

"Could he be single?" Sarah contemplated.

"Raymond was incredibly punctual, never once late for his appointments. It seems I'm fond of him. I understood it to be a platonic affection because falling in love with a stranger was foreign to me." She benumbed and paused.

"But can he still be considered a stranger?" she said raising her eyebrow.

"He's been doing so much for me; and I'll be graduating in a few months. He even assists me with my project, despite his busy schedule," Sarah admitted, a grin on her face.

"Stop daydreaming. Don't be foolish. He's already made it clear that we're siblings, and nothing indicates otherwise," she told herself, giving her cheek a light slap.

"Let me complete my studies and get to campus. Raymond will find something to eat when he comes" Sarah said running her left fingers through her hair.

"The fridge is stocked with plenty of food, and he'll know his way around the kitchen when he returns. I think I need to keep my feelings in check around him" she hissed fidgeting with a black pen.

"If he's genuinely interested, he'll invest time and attention," she concluded, smiling while she sent a text message.

2

Sometimes in life, we achieve through faith; that much is true, but without work, our hopes remain unfulfilled. The importance of something often becomes apparent only once we've lost it. Life, I believe, is inherently ambiguous.

It was during a break when Raymond decided to grab some lunch. Being a busy individual, he ensured things were done correctly. He glanced at his phone and noticed a message from Sarah.

"I'll be attending group studies and will be home late today. I've prepared your favorite dish in the fridge, hoping you'll enjoy it. Keep up the hard work, and thanks for the money you sent to my account," he read the message with a smile.

Things went smoothly between Sarah and Raymond until Sarah completed her studies. She was eager to do her national service at a mining firm, but Raymond urged her to work with him at his company.

"Being a service personnel or an intern and being retained after your service are two different things, my dear," he explained, gazing into her eyes.

"Did he just call me 'my dear'? Or did I mishear him?" she hissed.

"What happened to the usual 'sis' he calls me? Could he be developing feelings for me?" she wondered to herself.

"Sarah, are you paying attention?" Raymond asked to get her concentration.

"I have the influence to help you secure a job in the company, although not necessarily with the mining firm or any other organization" Raymond said looking straight into her eyes.

"While it may be lucrative, the question is 'who knows you?'" he asked and paused.

"Staying on in the workplace differs from moving from one office to another and garnering favor for employment," Raymond elaborated.

"My decision is made, and a friend has assured me of assistance in being retained after my national service" Sarah said with confidence.

"I know you want the best for me, but please allow me to make my own choice this time" Sarah said with ire in her eyes.

"Ever since you kindly offered to help me, you've been the one making decisions and finalizing choices," she responded with a hint of defiance in her tone.

Raymond was taken aback by her response, but before he could speak, Sarah interjected.

"Fred will be coming to collect my belongings for our place this Sunday. I apologize for the abrupt notice" Sarah said in a more heat than light.

"Our service is starting next Monday, and I need to settle in and prepare for the first day of work" she added and continued.

"He mentioned that the mining job is quite demanding, and I must be on my A-game," she finished, attempting to conclude the conversation.

Raymond found her revelation almost surreal, as he hadn't anticipated such news.

"Even if you intended to leave, an earlier notice would have been considerate" Raymond said politely.

"I genuinely had good intentions for you, but since you've made your choice, I have no objections. God knows my heart and the future I had envisioned for us," he reflected.

"I'll send you some money for your upkeep before you receive your first month's allowance," Raymond yelled from a distance.

"No need. Fred has assured me he'll take care of my needs once I'm at his place," she replied.

Fred was fair, tall, and muscular with well-shaped beard. He has been working at the mining firm as a drilling engineer for five years and was well known for his hard work. One evening, Sarah noticed that her acne cream had finished and decided to get a new one at a nearby cosmetic shop.

Upon reaching the entrance, she barged into Fred who was busy typing on his phone. He quickly apologized and offered to walk her home since it was late. At the gate, they exchanged contacts and kept in touch with each other. It was during one of their daily night conversations that Sarah got to know of his career which spiked her interest in the mining industry.

The period after this argument was all torn up. Raymond and Sarah, though they lived together, saw less of each other. Things seemed different and Sarah couldn't wait to leave the house and be rid of his presence.

Early Sunday morning, the doorbell rang, and it was Fred waiting to take Sarah to his home.

"Come on in. The door's opened. I'll be with you shortly," Sarah invited as she ushered Fred inside.

"Wow, this house is incredibly beautiful. I wish I could live here," Fred whispered to himself.

"Make yourself at home and feel comfortable. I'll be right there. I packed my things last week, but you'll need to help me load them into the car," Sarah said with a charming smile.

Fred continued to explore, marveling at the designs and exquisite fittings in the room. He looked around until he had nothing else to see. He tapped the chair and attempted to identify the manufacturer, but there was no label.

"This chair doesn't seem to be man-made. The cushion is so soft, you'd think you're sitting on clouds. There's happiness when you travel," he mused to himself.

A few minutes later, Sarah joined Fred, and he assisted in loading her belongings into the car.

"You've got quite a collection of dresses in there, and those bags are really nice," Fred complimented.

"Yes, Raymond buys them for me nearly every week and takes me shopping," she responded casually.

"Who...?" he asked straightforwardly.

"Raymond, of course. Who else?" she retorted.

"So, going to your place, we'll be shopping every day, right?" she quickly inquired.

"My place? Shopping every day?" Fred asked in amazement, coughing sarcastically.

"Oh, definitely! We'll do that if we can find a time after work," he replied, evading her curious gaze.

"Let's head to the house so I can unpack my things and rest for work" she said as she grabbed her handbag.

"I can't believe I'll also be working at the mine, meeting new people, and building a strong network for myself" Sarah happily leaped with a smile.

"Once I'm retained, I'll be enjoying some serious cash," she rambled as she browsed on her phone.

The car's engine roared back to life, marking the beginning of their journey. Conversations flowed as they shared their plans and dreams for the future. Sarah had ambitious aspirations, driven by her national service commitments. On the other hand, Fred was eager to reach home so he could make amends.

"Why is this network acting up?" she asked rhetorically.

"Since we started, I've sent numerous messages, all of which bounced back to me. I think I should switch to another SIM card," Sarah complained.

"Allow me to help. I discarded my own SIM card five months ago. Try using this one; it should resolve your issues and bring some perks your way," Fred joked as he handed his phone over to Sarah.

"If you need to send anything, feel free to use my phone. It's loaded with data," he added as he continued to drive.

"Wow! The message was sent so quickly. Raymond must have seen it by now," she exclaimed before returning the phone to Fred.

"What did you send him?" he inquired, curious.

"Nothing significant. I just let him know where he could find his keys when he gets home," she replied.

Meanwhile, Raymond was engrossed in work, searching for files for his upcoming presentation. Though he appeared concerned and heartbroken, the pressure at his desk demanded more attention than his emotions. He was devoted to his job, often sacrificing his personal life for it.

This dedication had propelled him from modest beginnings to success, earning him respect among prominent figures and the community. Even in failure, he believed one could triumph. When hope seemed lost, he offered faith as solace, mending the cracks in hope's foundation. In the face of death, he offered reassurance, even if it was based on a lie. This was who Raymond was.

Hours passed, and Raymond had completed his presentation, preparing to leave the office. He was known for being the last person to exit, even after the morning security guard. His colleagues often referred to him as "first-in, last-out," a title he took in stride as he fulfilled his responsibilities.

"So, was Sarah serious about her decision? Did I do something wrong?" Raymond said with his eyes opened wide.

"I was planning to propose to her next month, on her birthday. But such is life," he murmured as he realized he was alone in the office.

"Life can be unpredictable. What did I do to deserve this?" he questioned himself, a heavy sense of disappointment weighing on him.

Suddenly, he felt a presence behind him. It was the night security guard, Mr. Ameyaw, who was approaching him to get the keys of the building before Raymond left.

Mr. Ameyaw was dressed in an ash uniform stripped with black lines from the shoulder to the waist. He had his black beret on, while holding his long torch light with his old boots. His grey hair and soft speech gave him the popular nickname 'oluman' which means an old person. He stood akimbo with his protruded belly behind Raymond.

"Mr. Ameyaw, how long have you been standing there? Were you listening to me?" Raymond asked, slightly concerned.

"Sir ooh, no, of course not. How could I eavesdrop on my boss? I was on my way here and I heard you talking. I always knock before entering, just like the inscription on your door. But when I got closer, I noticed the door was already opened" he said seemingly tired.

"Sir ooh, I was about to knock, but... well, since it's almost the end of the month, if you'd like, you can give me half or no salary, like you did with the cleaner before. So, sir ooh…" Mr. Ameyaw hesitated.

"Why all this 'ooh' and 'ooh'? Can't you speak plain English without the 'ooh'?" Raymond asked, slightly amused.

"Sir, please don't be upset, ooh. If I don't add the 'ooh,' it feels like my sentences aren't complete," Mr. Ameyaw explained.

"Then why didn't you add 'ooh' to the last sentence you said?" Raymond questioned.

"Sorry, sir, the last statement was a metaphor, and when it ends like that, the 'ooh' comes from the listener. I was expecting you to add the 'ooh' to my statement. I've had this 'ooh' habit since primary school, but I'm sure I'll stop when the salary increases."

"Hahahaaa! Trying to outwit me, Mr. Ameyaw? Decisions on that matter are made by management. But please excuse me, I'll give you the keys after I finish sending some emails to our clients," Raymond replied.

"But sir ooh, what emails? Your computer is off, and your files are neatly arranged on the shelves. So, what emails are you sending?" Mr. Ameyaw giggled.

"Raymond, I'm three times your age, and I heard everything you said while fidgeting with your phone. What was her name… umm, Sarah…" Mr. Ameyaw revealed.

"Mr. Ameyaw, you won't understand the plans I had for her. My intentions were clear; my intentions were pure. My heart aches" he said as he beat his hand on his chest.

"I was waiting for the right moment, but she caught me off guard and left. You wouldn't understand unless you were in my shoes," Raymond lamented.

"Sir, I understand what you mean perfectly well. Sometimes, we might say 'let me tell you a story' when we're actually talking about ourselves. But in this case, it's the absolute truth about what happened to me," Mr. Ameyaw said, pulling up a chair to sit.

A long time ago, after leaving school with the belief that education wasn't the key, but intelligence was, I carried the burden of gossiping and stealing. I would talk about anything to gain favor and would spread lies to ruin the happiness in families, all for the sake of money or a simple thank-you as a form of recognition. Unbeknown to me, I was making life incredibly difficult for myself. At any hint of money, I was there to grab it before the owner could notice.

Ruining family happiness became my signature. I would go to great lengths to destroy the joy that couples had spent years building. Regardless of whether the information was true or false, I would spread it until marriages collapsed. That was who I was, Ameyaw. He told his story without a pause.

I could fabricate stories like…

"I saw your husband with a charming lady in his car. Judging by their conversation, I'm certain they're heading to the nearby hotel."

"Your wife has been lying about attending the all-night services. She's always in the pastor's room, and the noises that come from there are unbearable. You should consider leaving her before things get worse."

"Your wife confided in me that you're not satisfying her in bed, and she's much more content with a neighbor. She didn't just tell me; she told some friends too."

"Your husband has been secretly communicating with young girls and sends photos of nudity through his phone. He's being blackmailed that's why he always complains about money. All the money he gets, he sends it to the young girl."

Ameyaw added…

I fabricated these stories and countless others to break apart peaceful families.

I was sentenced to three years in prison, though I managed to get out early. At the police station, I stole the money that had been given as a bribe. That money saved me from having to walk the distance to a place I didn't even know. I lost everything and became a beggar.

"But Mr. Ameyaw, what does this have to do with the heartbreak I'm experiencing?" Raymond asked confused.

"Even if it relates to relationships, I don't see how stealing, prison, and gossip fit into the picture. I can't find any connection to what I'm going through," Raymond interjected still confused.

"So, since you don't see a connection between what I'm saying and your worries, do you only focus on things that directly concern your life?" Mr. Ameyaw asked concerned.

"Don't you realize that you could become a victim in some way sooner or later?" he asked, pausing for emphasis.

"But I don't see how my worry is related. I don't engage in stealing, gossiping, or being imprisoned. I believe a certain level of concern is healthy, but within limits," Raymond explained.

"Sir, even if nobody technically owns it, you stole something you hadn't paid for. The pain you're feeling might be because you've contributed significantly to her success, or because she lived with you, or more likely, a combination of both."

"Both? You're right. But how did you know?" Raymond inquired, clearly surprised.

"The distance the elderly can see while sitting, a young person can't see even if they climb the highest mountain in the world," he replied, allowing another pause.

"Sir, even keeping a charming lady in your house can lead to accusations of theft, even if the person has lost her parents. She has extended family members who might be waiting for a chance to accuse you. You might not engage in gossip, but that won't necessarily protect you from legal repercussions. Your good intentions might not matter in the court of law. The court focuses on the law and actions, not intentions or truth. What does the law state, and how is it applied? That's what determines the final verdict," Mr. Ameyaw advised.

"Consider yourself fortunate that she left with short notice. What if she had left suddenly after a month or two? Would you have changed her plans? The Bible teaches us that God's plans for us surpass our imagination and understanding. While you may have your own plans, remember that God's ways are not our ways, and His thoughts are not our thoughts," he added, and Raymond nodded in agreement.

"After facing my own challenges in life, I found a better path for myself. It hasn't been easy, but at least I don't steal from people. I work for one of the largest companies in the world as a security guard. I've traded my sleep for a paycheck, and any negligence on my part could have significant consequences for the company."

"The critical point is that I'll be retiring soon. My firstborn is ten years old, and my youngest is just a baby. My wife is pregnant, and times are tough. If you can't emulate the Apostle Paul from the Holy

Bible, then I urge you to marry early. Holding onto the idea of having plans for a woman can hinder you from starting a family and can even undermine your goals. Marry when you find a woman and work together to shape each other. There's no perfect woman; you make her perfect."

"Sir ooh, I'd say that God wants what's best for you. He allowed these events to unfold for a reason. It's painful to let go of something you've invested in, but in doing so, you'll realize that God has something special in store for you. I must get to the gate to deter potential thieves. My livelihood depends on this job, and my children rely on me to provide for our household," he concluded, making his way out of the office.

"There's an incongruence between my feelings and his long story. Haa…! Old men" Raymond said as he packed out of the office.

"Let's go to a hotel for lunch. I am starving. We can even stay the night and head home tomorrow. My house is just a short distance from here," Fred suggested.

"Why not? Let's go. I'm quite hungry too, and I'm surprised you noticed. We seem to have something in common, I suppose," Sarah chimed in.

"Absolutely! It feels like we share a lot in common" Fred added.

"Working at the same company is a good indicator. We'll have plenty to talk about, you know? Staying together will be like being a couple, and I'm looking forward to sleeping next to you," Fred grinned.

Sarah didn't respond; she assumed he would repeat himself. However, Fred ignored her silence and drove to the hotel. They ordered food and drinks, engaged in light-hearted banter, and discussed the challenges people faced in earning a living. The conversation took an interesting turn when they delved into the topic of the government's e-levy policy.

Even the waitress who brought them a bottle of water lamented the impact of the e-levy, expressing how it had significantly affected her income.

"Mr. and Mrs., this government has truly let us down. Now, my boyfriends who used to send me money are using the e-levy as an excuse to avoid sending money as they usually do. I hardly even touched my salary, but now, with the e-levy deductions, our paychecks are shrinking," she vented.

"So, how many boyfriends do you have?" Sarah inquired, a hint of curiosity in her voice.

"Madam, boyfriends? I have more than I can count. Men always want to explore, so I offer myself to them in exchange for what I desire" the waitress replied, throwing her fingers in the air.

"You know that one woman isn't enough for a man, and I'm there to fulfill those needs, getting my desires met. You scratch my back, and I scratch yours. And I even …" the waitress was interrupted.

"Excuse me, I hear the man in black short sleeve shirt calling for your attention," Fred quickly interjected, diverting the conversation.

The waitress moved to attend to the other table.

"She was about to reveal something, and you interrupted. Why would a young woman think this way? Is this the norm of our youth? Who's influencing today's generation?" Sarah asked Fred.

"Did you notice something?"

"The tall man in black just gave her money and his business card," she pointed out, indicating their direction.

"Many young women nowadays seem to seek an easy path to prosperity. Reaping where you haven't sown always comes at a price. I recall what my late uncle told me about the consequences of evil deeds," Fred said, while gazing at the chicken soup.

"Evil actions will take you further than you intended to go; they will cost you more than you were willing to pay, and they will keep you longer than you were prepared to stay," he added.

Sarah had him repeat the statement until she fully grasped it. She requested examples to help her understand better and to educate those who were straying.

"Someone involved in corporate fraud may intend to make a quick profit but find themselves embroiled in a complex web of deceit and illegal activities that extend far beyond their initial intentions. They may end up facing severe legal penalties and losing their reputation" Fred explained as he gulped down his juice.

"A person who engages in an extramarital affair might think it's a short-term fling without serious consequences. However, it can lead to broken relationships, emotional turmoil, and long-lasting damage to personal and family life" he further explained.

"Posting offensive or harmful content on social media may seem like a minor action, but it can quickly escalate. Such behavior can lead to public outrage, damage to one's online reputation, and even legal repercussions" Fred rebuked.

"Thus, very inspiring. You are very smart, and I love your sense of intelligence" Sarah said marveled.

"I'm not done with the examples. You need to share this quote with anyone" Fred added and continued.

"Someone who tells a lie to cover up a small mistake may find themselves having to tell more lies to maintain the deception. This can spiral out of control, leading to a loss of trust and credibility in their personal and professional life" Sarah sat amused in a straight face as Fred talked.

"Starting to use drugs or alcohol recreationally may be intended for temporary enjoyment. However, addiction can take individuals much further than they intended, resulting in physical and mental health issues, financial ruin, and strained relationships."

"Politicians who engage in corrupt practices to gain power or financial advantages can quickly find themselves involved in a web of corruption that extends beyond their initial intentions. This can lead to scandals, legal consequences, and damage to their political careers" Fred added and paused.

3

Wise individuals value advice and remain indifferent to its source or the person from whom it originates. Valuable lessons can be discovered amidst the tumultuous winds of life's storms.

Sarah and Fred finally arrived at the house. The expression on Sarah's face showed she was disappointed and burdened. She appeared weighed down with thoughts, and Fred anticipated a barrage of questions. However, she remained silent.

"Come to think of it, Fred mentioned he wanted to confess something to me. Is this what's bothering him?" Sarah wondered aloud as she went out to retrieve the last bag.

"You can take a seat. I know..." Fred bagged in being interrupted by Sarah.

"Yes, your house might not be lavish, but your heart is as good as gold. What truly matters is having a place to lay our heads, and your bed is more than sufficient for both of us. A modest single room is manageable. I was homeless before I met Raymond, and he offered me shelter. I believe that life must go on, regardless of the success or wealth he possesses. Who knows if it's ill-gotten gains?" Sarah interjected.

"Ill-gotten gains? Could luxurious houses and cars really be the result of harming others? Can people be so heartless as to take innocent lives for their own benefit?" Fred asked, genuinely taken aback.

"Well, if you don't realize the cruelty that exists in our world, then you're not paying attention. People can be ruthless and indifferent to the suffering of others. I've witnessed a lot in life, although I don't think that money rituals are a widespread issue in this country," Sarah clarified.

Fred was left in disbelief after hearing such statements from Sarah. Despite her sharing her own story, he still found it baffling why she had stayed with Raymond for so long. It remained a mystery to him, and he struggled to understand why she chose to follow him to this rented house.

"My brother will be arriving from Kumasi soon, and he'll be using his car until he leaves," Fred mentioned.

"The car isn't yours? But you previously said the car was yours, and that you worked at the mine," Sarah questioned, clearly surprised.

"I never said I didn't work at the mine" Fred almost burst out.

"We'll be taking the bus to work tomorrow, so you'll see for yourself. I'm quite tired and need to shower before retiring to bed. You can join me after that," Fred yawned before heading to the bathroom.

"Did I make the right choice by leaving Raymond's house? He never spoke to me like this during our time together. Our time there was peaceful, but Fred's words are baffling. However, he promised to help me secure a job at the mine," Sarah pondered as she undressed.

Meanwhile Raymond left the office and headed home, radiating happiness. He played gospel music in his car, singing along joyfully. Within an hour, he reached his house and remembered the message Sarah sent about where she had kept the key the previous day. He retrieved the key which was hidden under the electricity generator he uses in his home. A smile appeared on his face when he found the key exactly where she had left it. In that moment, he realized how much he missed her presence and felt a sense of loneliness.

Raymond took the key, inserted it into the door, and turned it three times until it finally opened. He rubbed his legs on the doormat and walked inside, turning on the light in the living room.

Sitting on the chair, and thinking about Sarah's leaving, he remembered a story that was shared by an old man.

The story revolved around a very poor woman with a small family who had called a radio station seeking help from God. A non-believer had listened to the call and decided to mock the woman. He obtained her address and instructed his secretary to buy and deliver a variety of groceries to her.

"If the woman asks who sent the food, tell her it's from the devil," he instructed.

When the secretary arrived at the woman's house, the woman was overwhelmed with gratitude for the unexpected assistance. The secretary assisted in organizing the groceries in her small refrigerator.

"Don't you want to know who sent the food?" the secretary inquired after waiting for a while.

"No, please convey my gratitude to whoever sent this! I'm not concerned about the sender's identity. When God commands, even the devil obeys," the woman replied.

The old man had shared this story with him, advising him to reflect on its meaning. So, he saw that Sarah's leaving was something he had to accept.

"In the Bible the account about Hannah's pregnancy was a miracle, but it took nine months, just like any other pregnancy. God's plans don't negate the significance of the process. Sometimes, waiting is a necessary part of the journey. I will wait and seek understanding," he encouraged himself, said a prayer, and drifted off to sleep.

Early in the morning the following day, Raymond bumped into Mr. Ameyaw while lost in his thoughts, on the way to his office.

"I thought I could fight my own battles, but the advice you gave me has started to heal my wounds. Thank you very much for the insightful advice. I haven't had anyone speak to me like this in my entire life. I want to give you something for your family tomorrow. Although what I have right now isn't much," Raymond said, his tone filled with gratitude.

"Sir ooh, thank you very much. But please, I hope it's not a cash advance, because I'm aware of what you are capable of, you know. My family is already grateful for your kindness, even before I've received anything. Please don't change your mind, as I've already spent the money. I owe a lot of people, and I owe myself. This life I've built for myself isn't easy, but I have faith that God will provide a way," Mr. Ameyaw cheerfully responded.

"Hahaha... You always manage to bring a smile to people's faces and help them forget their worries. I truly appreciate the advice, and I intend to fulfill my part of our arrangement. Let's meet before you close from work tomorrow morning," Raymond said, sharing a laugh.

"But have you taken your wife to the hospital for a check-up to determine the gender of your unborn child?" Raymond inquired with genuine concern.

"The gender of my unborn child? I don't think it's a priority for me right now" Mr. Ameyaw chuckled.

"We struggle to even have three square meals a day, so spending money to find out the gender of the baby doesn't seem necessary. I'm ready for whatever God blesses us with. Sometimes these scans can be misleading," Mr. Ameyaw explained.

"Well, you do have a point, but what if I provide you with some money for the check-up?" Raymond suggested.

"I would be grateful to accept, and I'll keep track of the expenses to report back to you. Accountability is important for someone who's responsible. God bless you for your thoughtfulness towards my family," Mr. Ameyaw responded.

"Don't mention it... Have a wonderful day,"

"This old man can talk for Ghana. I wonder why he is misusing his talent by working as a security guard" Raymond continued, mumbling to himself.

The morning was bright, and Sarah's face was lit up with happiness. As previously arranged, Fred accompanied her to work, and she began her role as a national service person. They had to part ways, as Fred was part of the drilling and blasting team in the mining company, while Sarah had to go through series of induction before she was rotated through the various sections in the department.

Sarah enjoyed her first day on the job, and her colleagues appreciated her sense of humor and willingness to help. She eagerly took on errands and assisted with tasks.

"Given her enthusiasm, she might get tired of the general national service meetings quickly. It was quite shocking when they straightforwardly informed us that there won't be any employment opportunities soon. It's a harsh truth, but we're still hopeful for a positive change. Hopefully, a miracle will happen," a short guy whispered to his friend.

"The same way our seniors told us. Ruth and Mercy had the opportunity to work here after their service, but none of the guys did. I see a high chance of her being retained. Never underestimate the power of a woman," his friend added.

"Well, what you're saying is true. She even came here with an employee reference. She has connections and a strong network. I suggest we befriend her to learn more about her," the short guy responded.

"Even the Bible says, 'The way to a man's heart is through his stomach,'" his friend added with a chuckle.

"That's in the Bible, but I don't think you're interpreting it quite right. Your suggestion is excellent, and I believe befriending her could increase our chances of getting employed after our national service," his friend said thoughtfully.

During the break, Sarah had become well-known among her colleagues. She found it hard to stay seated, as she wanted to capture everyone's attention. She even helped the cafeteria staff tidy up and serve desserts.

"Who's she? She's stunningly beautiful. I love her figure. Just the way I prefer, unlike my wife. My village deities must have been sleeping when they gave me my wife. She can't even give me a child," one coworker remarked.

"She's one of the current national service personnel. You can ask Fred about her; they live in the same area. But it's true, the most beautiful ones are yet to be born. Marrying at twenty-seven caused your own problems; now deal with it," his friend teased.

"Don't mock me over a mere woman. My parents, who pressured me into marrying at that age, are now deceased, and I'm suffering. I never managed to convince them that I was too young for marriage; they insisted on seeing their grandchildren before they died…"

"Did they live to see them?" his friend interjected with a grin.

"Maybe they're content with their grandchildren in the afterlife. Whenever I see my wife, I remember my parents' words, especially my mother's."

"What words? 'If you don't marry her, you're no longer my son'?" his friend asked.

"Exactly!!! How did you know? Can you read minds now? Then read her mind and tell me… what's her name again?"

"Sarah? Forget about her. You're a married man, and you should honor your vows. My mother also used those words on me, but my younger sister advised me to move out and stay with friends to ease the tension. The funny part was, I wasn't allowed to choose my own partner; I had to accept the woman my mother was determined to give me," his friend explained.

"The same happened to me, and now this marriage ring is squeezing me tighter. I want to divorce her for Sarah. I'm sure my true children are meant to be with Sarah. She's incredibly beautiful and caring. Look at the way she's eating. I need to get her number before the day ends."

"My friend, you're taking on more than you can handle. Focus on your marriage and pray for it. The same God you approached at the altar with your wife is still there, ready to listen to your prayers and turn things around. Your eyes are always wandering, seeking out innocent women to prey on. Until you shift your gaze to Jesus, you'll never see anything of value in your wife," his friend advised.

"Since you see the beauty in her, why don't you go for her yourself? I won't charge you a dime. So, when are you planning to make your move?" his friend asked.

"I can't quite figure out what kind of person she is. She talks and complains about everything to her friends and family. We have no secrets we can call our own. If she's not the devil, she must be related to one," his friend added.

"I'll marry your wife only if you invite the same people who witnessed your wedding to witness your divorce. You can officially tell them why you're leaving her in front of everyone, just like you did with your marriage vows. Then I'll gladly marry her and even cover the costs of your entire wedding," his friend said.

"If that's your plan, then let me live my life. You just told me to heal my wounds, right? That's exactly what I'm doing, so please, Mr. Fortune Teller, let me be," he retorted before leaving the table.

His friend was surprised that he could consider leaving the woman he had paid a bride price for simply because she hadn't given birth and wasn't conventionally beautiful. Parents can sometimes be a source of frustration. Especially for firstborns, they often push for a legacy that aligns with their desires, often based on their interpretation of what's right. When you attempt to deviate, they can use Bible verses to compel obedience to parental authority.

While obedience is important, it can also be unreasonable and exasperating. However, having a listening ear to parental expectations are necessary.

"I believe marriage is a lifelong journey without turning back. So, for me, age isn't the issue. It's about understanding the complexities of marriage, knowing how to maintain a home and family. That's the right foundation for marriage, in my opinion," he concluded before heading back to work.

Raymond had returned to his office after giving the money he promised to Mr. Ameyaw. He had previously admired Rita at the office for a long time, but his interest had waned when Sarah came into the picture. Rita was exceptionally beautiful and intelligent. She reported directly to Raymond, and her attire was always impeccable. Despite her modest salary, she treated everyone with respect and carried out her tasks diligently and passionately. Her integrity was something to be admired.

"I need to get Rita's attention. I think she might be interested in me too. She'd make a perfect partner, with her looks, height, and smile. I'm sure my friends will like her as well. I should act quickly before someone else catches her eye. But what if she's already in a relationship? What if I propose and she rejects me?"

"That would be embarrassing, and the headlines would be brutal. 'Secretary Rejects Boss's Marriage Proposal.' I can't bear the shame that would bring, and the worst part would be having to ask her to keep it confidential. That's usually impossible for women," he thought to himself.

"What can I do to avoid this humiliation?" Raymond mused, pen in hand.

Raymond was contemplating how to win Rita's heart, even though he had documents to read, comprehend, and sign. He read a few lines, then pondered what actions to take, rereading the same lines repeatedly.

"I should start by showering her with gifts. I'm confident she'll get the message and eventually accept my proposal. But I need to be sure she's single, or history might repeat itself, like in the seventies," he reasoned and focused on his work.

"Mr. Boss, I only wanted to inform you that my credit is running low. Don't worry; I'll give you the information you need about this young lady. She's a hard nut to crack, but I'm sure you can handle her," Ama, Rita's best friend informed Raymond after he enquired about winning Rita's heart.

"Thank you, Ama. I appreciate your help. Please, let me know if there are any updates," Raymond said before ending the call.

As he walked out of the restaurant, Raymond thought about how challenging it was going to be to get close to Rita. But he was determined not to give up. He knew that with the right approach, he could eventually break down the walls she had built around herself. He hailed a taxi and headed back to his office, his mind full of thoughts about Rita and the steps he needed to take to win her over.

Ama did her best to talk to Rita regarding Raymonds interest. Rita thought over it severally, finding answers to questions. After days of discussions, she decided to give in and see the outcome.

Raymond had successfully captured Rita's heart, and their relationship blossomed. A devout Christian, Rita attended church without fail. She was well-mannered and raised by uneducated but well-intentioned parents. Rita consistently invited Raymond to accompany her to church unless he was swamped with work.

At this point, they were both ready to get married and had informed the church pastor.

This practice fostered a loving and heartwarming relationship between them. The church pastor and elders noticed their attendance and, more notably, Raymond's financial support.

One evening, the pastor summoned Raymond and Rita to his office for a discussion.

"I'm not sure I'm ready to take on the role of a church elder. My work schedule won't allow it. Juggling both responsibilities might lead me to an early grave. Whenever you're called, you need to drop everything and go," Raymond lamented as he and Rita made their way to the pastor's office.

"Whatever God bestows upon a person; He also grants the knowledge and strength to fulfill it. Although we don't know the specifics of why the pastor wants to see us, I don't think becoming a church elder would be impossible. Do your part and trust God with the rest. He will guide your path and won't lead you to your demise. I'll support you when I'm available. For now, let's hear what the pastor has in mind," Rita reassured him.

As they entered the pastor's office, they were offered seats and politely declined the offer of water, having recently had some.

"Let's begin with a prayer. Sister Rita, would you lead us in prayer?" the pastor suggested.

"Dear Lord Jesus, please preside over our conversation and guide us to a fruitful resolution. Bless us and the church. Amen," Rita prayed, and they all echoed, "Amen."

4

Love and romance are often interconnected but carry distinct meanings. You can reflect on both and explore their relationship. Love is the foundation, while romance adds a special touch if you're seeking to express that love.

"I've called you here for a specific reason. I'm pleased to see how well your relationship is progressing, and I advise you to expedite the necessary preparations before temptation leads you astray" Pastor said respectfully to them.

"Together with the Elders, we're offering our prayers and support to help you become the couple you aspire to be," the pastor stated, pausing for emphasis.

"Elder Sey will oversee any counseling required. He'll guide you with essential information regarding your preparations" he added and paused.

"We've observed within the church that some men are taking advantage of women. Some of these women are growing older without getting married, often because some men have deceived them with promises of marriage and then left them" Elder Sey said looking at their faces.

"Consequently, they're left waiting for suitors who never come. These men often communicate among themselves, deterring other men from considering the women they've taken advantage of " he added as he took a sheet of paper from the printer.

"As a result, no one is willing to marry these women because they've been abandoned" the pastor said tapping his pen.

"Starting with you, we're committed to resolving any obstacles you may encounter, ensuring that you're mentally, physically, and emotionally prepared for marriage" the pastor said clasping hands together.

"However, if there's any significant issue that contradicts biblical teachings or has health implications, making it inappropriate to bless your union, we may advise separation. This would be communicated sensitively to the church," Elder Sey added.

"From this point on, you must abstain from any intimacy or actions that could arouse sexual desires" the pastor said as Raymond crossed his legs.

"We're serious about this, and I'll be observant. The church will be officially informed next Sunday as our doctrines require" the pastor added as Rita looked at Raymond.

"If you have questions, feel free to ask, and kindly provide your contact numbers on the sheet of paper in front of you," Elder Sey requested.

"Thank you, pastor, and the elders, for taking this initiative. We're grateful that you've chosen to support us in this journey" Raymond said smirking.

"We're committed to maintaining our chastity until our wedding day, as we've already planned. Thank you once again," Raymond expressed, while Rita jotted down her number.

"We'll do our best to honor the reputation of the church, as others may not have. Please keep us in your prayers," Rita added, handing the paper to the pastor.

"Rita, you remembered his number off the top of your head? That's quite remarkable and shows the depth of your affection. It took me months to memorize my wife's number. Not that I didn't love her, but I never saw the need, as I always had my phone with me," the pastor commented, surprised.

Raymond frequently checked the time because he had an upcoming appointment. Rita had left her job due to her relationship with Raymond. Despite her strong dedication to her work, she resigned to focus on the marriage preparations, as tradition dictated.

"As you have no further questions, make sure you adhere to everything I've shared. Before you go,

Raymond, please offer a prayer on our behalf," the pastor requested.

"Shall we pray?" Raymond asked.

They all stood up with their heads bowed down and Raymond whispered a prayer saying;

"Heavenly Father, we thank you for this productive discussion. It's by your grace and divine mercy that we've come this far in our journey. We ask for your continued favor as we prepare to become a united couple. As we depart from here but not from your presence, we pray for your continued blessings upon us and all members of the church. Bless us now and forevermore in the name of your Son, Jesus. Amen."

"Amen," they responded together.

"Your prayers are quite moving. You could consider becoming an elder in the church. Pray and think about it," the pastor suggested.

"Elder?" they both exclaimed.

"Yes, give it some thought. Rita, you have the demeanor of an elder's wife. Your smile could inspire the younger women, and your presence would set an example for the young ladies. You would be a wonderful figure to guide the younger generation," the pastor said with evident joy.

"We'll take some time to consider and provide you with our response. We appreciate your suggestion, but we need time to give you an answer," Rita responded while Raymond nodded in affirmation.

Leaving the pastor's office, they found it somewhat amusing that such a compliment came at an unexpected time. Sometimes, we might hear messages from God, but if we don't engage in frequent communion with Him, we might mistake His voice for other unrelated thoughts. Discerning the true nature of these moments can be challenging, especially when we're not attuned to them. Time often plays a crucial role in the decisions we make.

Life continued, and mining work remained challenging. Yet, Sarah and Fred persevered, sustained by grace. Six months passed without major issues. Sarah developed a circle of friends among the managers, and she was often absent from home. Fred was deeply interested in her, but he faced stiff competition.

Late one night, Sarah was awakened by a disturbance outside her window. Struggling to open her eyes, she felt an irresistible urge to return to sleep. However, the noise persisted, preventing her from drifting off.

"I regret the day I allowed you into my life as my husband."

"Who convinced me to be with you in the first place? You're nothing but a thorn in my side. I loathe calling you my wife. The moment you entered my life, everything fell apart."

"Are you even a man? You sleep and snore like a goat in line for a vaccine. I despise the day I allowed you into my bed. I didn't derive any pleasure from you at all. Look at who's claiming to be a man."

"Fred, wake up and listen to what's happening. Our neighbors next door are fighting," Sarah said, tapping him.

"You mean Collins and Betty?"

"Yes..."

"Unbelievable. Aren't they the couple who got married a few months ago? We should listen carefully before jumping to conclusions. It's late, and we can't intervene," Fred advised, astonished.

"You'll pay for every cent I've invested in you for telling me I'm not a man. You despicable woman from nowhere. I made you a woman, and now you dare speak to me with such disrespect. Who's the father of our three-weeks-old baby?" Collins said in an angry tone.

"Even if I've given birth, does that make you any more of a man? That's your child lying there. I detest you for the rest of my life." Betty shouted while fixing the cloth tired around her waist.

"Why is Betty speaking to her husband like that? Is that what marriage has come to? I've known them for over three years, and they were so happy while dating. They shared everything. I even used to call them Romeo and Juliet," Fred said in surprise.

"I just can't comprehend the chemistry behind a long-lasting relationship. When it transforms into marriage, it can stir up quite a commotion among the same lovers. This marks the fifth time I've witnessed such a marital dispute," Sarah said with amusement.

"First thing tomorrow morning, I'm sending you back to your family. I've had enough of your insults. I know this baby isn't mine. The day he was born, he didn't seem thrilled to see me. He had his little fist clenched and didn't open it. I'm sure he wanted to give me a good knock," Collins exclaimed in frustration.

"Why wouldn't he give you a knock? He probably realized you didn't contribute enough to make him look good and especially resemble you. Don't even think about kicking my things out of this house. Who pays the rent and the utility bills here? Remember, I rented this place after your lease expired," Betty retorted.

"But how can the clenching of a baby's hand determine his biological father? Lack of knowledge, Collins, that's your downfall," Fred chimed in, bursting into laughter.

"But why aren't you married?" Sarah inquired.

"Marriage? I don't think it's in my blood" Fred answered.

"I want to be like Paul from the Holy Bible. Although marriage has its blessings, I don't believe it's obligatory for everyone. Did you know that in Heaven, we'll be individuals and not married couples? I mean, you wouldn't recognize someone as your spouse?" Fred explained.

"Are you saying there's no marriage in Heaven? That can't be true! Why did God even create marriage if it won't exist in the afterlife? Why do we bother with marriage on Earth?" Sarah asked incredulously.

"In Heaven, there's no marriage. You can ask your pastor these questions. Since he's more closely connected to God, he might have some answers. As for me, the answers I've sought seem distant from my relationship with God," Fred replied.

"Now we can finally sleep peacefully. They've stopped fighting. Don't meddle in lovers' affairs. First, there's a fight, and then comes the moments of enjoyment," Sarah remarked.

A few minutes later...
"Can't we enjoy our sleep in peace? After that intense fight, now..." Sarah began.

"What's happening now? Do you have your ears in everyone's room? Can't you focus on your sleep? You're disturbing me," Fred grumbled.

"Just because you sleep like a pregnant ant, you think everyone sleeps like you, huh? Just listen..." Sarah retorted; frustration evident in her tone.

"Listen to what at this hour? I have a lot to tackle at work tomorrow, and I can't sacrifice my sleep for everything I hear," Fred replied.

"Don't I also have to go to work? What if armed robbers are breaking into our room? Just because you don't have anything valuable here, you think I'll risk my life?" Sarah shot back.

"What! Armed robbers? What did we do? Where are they?" Fred exclaimed, quickly getting up from his bed.

"Just listen, and you'll figure out who the 'armed robbers' are," Sarah answered.

"Kill me, kill me, kill me!" the moaning continued to escalate.

"Moaning in tears."

"You're making my night. So, when will I see you after today?" the man's voice inquired.

"Um… I'll be back. You're my best client ever," came the reply.

"That's Francis," Fred said, turning over to sleep.

"And the woman screaming, disturbing our sleep? Was she taught that during her counseling?"

"That lady isn't his wife. She's a nighttime worker. Francis's wife only left yesterday," Fred clarified.

"Yesterday…? And he couldn't even wait for his wife? Are you sure we should trade our peaceful single lives for marriage? This neighborhood is full of surprises," Sarah exclaimed.

"You haven't seen anything yet. Just wait until Yakubu returns from his father's funeral. You'll hear the real noise. He sleeps with anyone in skirts, regardless of age," Fred said, trying to coax himself back to sleep.

"Then I'll find a new place for myself. I've saved up a bit, and I can rent my own place. This place is absolutely dreadful. I need to start my search before this Yakubu guy comes back," Sarah declared, burying herself in an attempt to sleep.

Rita and Raymond on the phone...

"I'm missing you, my love, and I can't wait to be with you. Aside from not being by your side all the time, hearing your voice gives me butterflies, and it's as if I rule the world. I love you deeply," Rita said in a soft tone as she rolled herself on the bed.

"I love you more than you can fathom. I'm impatient to hold you close. Knowing you has transformed my life. I was searching blindly, but now I've found gold." Raymond added licking his soft pink lips.

"Love, when can we plan a trip out of the country or to a distant place? Rita asked pulling the bedsheet onto herself.

"And have you thought of what the pastor said about becoming a church Elder?" Rita inquired dancing her legs in the bedsheets.

"Why do you keep asking me this? Raymond wondered seeking for an answer.

"I've already told you I'm not interested in taking the role of a church elder. It's demanding and exhausting, and it often leaves church members unsatisfied. Moreover, some disrespect the woman you marry," Raymond explained.

"It's getting late, and we should sleep. About the business venture we discussed, let's finalize the details during lunchtime to turn this dream into reality. I believe you have the potential to be a successful businesswoman, and I'll support you in every way I can," he added without talking about the trip.

"Thank you for your unwavering support. You'll always be my favorite and my love. I'll let you rest now. I have a free day tomorrow, so I can catch up on sleep," Rita said while holding the pillow closer to her chest.

They shared a brief prayer before ending the call and Raymond drifted off to sleep.

5

We only have one life and one body to take care of, so it is imperative that we do so correctly. We never know what tomorrow may bring, so it's important to make the most out of each day and be grateful for everything we have.

Early in the morning, the day was bright, and everyone was busy making work plans. Time was passing quickly, and there was a queue at the bathhouse. Sarah couldn't stop complaining about the unfavorable treatment Fred had given her. She kept mentioning Raymond's name and how well he had treated her. Fred wasn't in a great mood, but he remained silent.

"Until I teach Sarah a valuable lesson, she won't respect me," Fred muttered to himself while angrily adjusting the towel around his waist.

Tenants had their buckets of water lined up in front of the bathhouse. Fred was next in line after Sarah who was getting ready to enter the bathhouse. The earlier person bathing was stepping out fully covered in her morning cloth, with her towel on her shoulder.

"Both of you can take a bath together since you share the same room," a fellow tenant behind Fred suggested.

The expressions on Sarah's face conveyed all the information the tenant needed. Fred secretly hoped the tenant would insist that they bathe together to save time, but she didn't pursue the matter further.

Fred wasn't pleased with Sarah's behavior, but he also had his own plans. He had made several attempts to catch a glimpse of Sarah's thigh, but he had been consistently denied.

Fred thought he could not spend on her so easily. He needed to have his way with her before she leaves his house. Fred knew Sarah was not someone to let go of easily and was ready to either grope or resort to other methods. That was what he had vowed to himself.

The world we inhabit can be quite cruel, and people rarely do things without an ulterior motive. Even couples keep a tally of each other's good deeds in case they need to demand something in a minor disagreement. Understanding people's true intentions is incredibly challenging. They might seem to love you wholeheartedly, but in reality, they might be the ones inflicting wounds that are hard to heal.

Meanwhile, Raymond was filled with happiness, evident in his smiles. It had been years since he had a long conversation with a woman over the phone. He wished that tomorrow was the day of his wedding. Upon reaching the office, he said his usual prayer and took a seat.

"Who's there? Come in," he called out when someone knocked on the door.

"Ah, Mr. Ameyaw, please have a seat. How are you doing?" Raymond greeted as he entered.

"I'm doing well, but I'll be doing even better if you could spare me some coins to buy porridge this morning. I haven't eaten since yesterday," Mr. Ameyaw explained looking sad.

"Make yourself comfortable" he said with a smile, pointing his right hand to the chair directly in front of him.

"You'll have breakfast with me today, and any other day I'm around," Raymond said, heading to get some hot water.

"Breakfast every day? That's fantastic news. I'm guessing a salary raise is on the horizon," Mr. Ameyaw said excitedly.

"Actually, breakfast is only for today. I've changed my mind."

"Oh, Boss, don't do me like this ooh. I was just joking" he said scratching his head.

"But how is Rita? I miss her a lot. She's been giving me leftovers every afternoon, but with you, I need to ask. Treat me kindly; I have grand plans for you," Mr. Ameyaw playfully stated.

"Send your breakfast away and please keep the cup and spoon. I need to call my beloved angel" Raymond said picking his phone.

"I miss her dearly and can't wait to hear her voice," he added with a smile.

"Boss, if I may ask ooh, please don't get angry. Do you ever miss Sarah too?" Mr. Ameyaw inquired after quickly grabbing the food tray with a cup full of cocoa beverage and a full loaf of hot brown-bread.

"Sarah is my past, and I don't dwell on the past in my life. I believe in building a successful future rather than allowing my past to haunt me. Yes, there are memories of her, but they don't hold any special place in my life," Raymond explained.

"You've always been a role model for strength to me. Do you know that many people in this office look up to you? It's not just because you're the boss, but because you're a go-getter and your level of intelligence is outstanding," Mr. Ameyaw praised him with his left foot adjusted to the door.

"Thank you very much for your kind words. Now, if you'll excuse me, I have work to attend to. Please extend my regards to your family when you get home," Raymond added dialing Rita's number the second time.

"I know you're pushing me away because you want to call your lover, Rita. But don't forget to tell her that if she can't give me leftovers, she can at least send me some cash," Mr. Ameyaw joked as he left the office.

Raymond and Rita on the phone...
"Hello, my love, how are you?" Raymond said with a broad smile, tilting his chair backwards.

"I'm doing very well, by the grace of God. Thank you so much for the money you sent. May God bless you." Rita happily replied, taking the phone from her ear after hearing a call beep.

"I'm glad to hear you're feeling good today. What do you want?" Raymond asked cheerfully.

"I want a guy who can truly see me. Someone who will love me so deeply that I won't be afraid to reveal my flaws. I want him to show me scars I never knew existed" Rita replied.

"And I don't want him to make those scars disappear. I want him to hold my hand as I heal them myself" Rita paused licking her lips.

"And I want him to cherish the marks they leave behind," Rita said, her voice softening.

"That's really touching. Many would ask for money, houses, cars, and more, but your request is something I'll gladly honor" Raymond responded piqued.

"What I want from you is to be with me completely, with your heart and mind," he added.

Later, Sarah reached the security post, where a young man called out to her. Initially resistant, she turned to see who was calling after a whisper from her friend. Sarah and the young man had a brief conversation before she hurried back to the security post.

"You're cleared now. Have a good morning, Miss Sarah," the security guard informed her slightly bowing down his head.

"How did the security guard know your name?" her friend asked startled.

"I don't know, my dear. I'm not surprised he mentioned my name. I might be even more popular than the managing director of the company," she said, and they all laughed.

"What did he say to you?" her friend inquired eagerly.

"Liza, you're really curious. Mind your own business," Sarah responded bluntly.

Liza paused for a moment, took a deep breath, and walked away in a different direction. She found Sarah's behavior quite amusing and whispered to herself until she reached her office.

Sometimes, the way we express our love can heal relationship wounds more effectively than we can imagine. Letting go of our ego and pride can take us far in the realm of love wherever we wish to go. There are times when we doubt our love for each other, but when we genuinely open our hearts, we find a skilled healer for our wounds.

A company-wide announcement was made about the latest changes in the company. It concerned a significant downsizing. The list of affected employees was extensive, and emotions ran high. Eyes were red with anger, and the national service personnel seemed unfazed since their fate was already decided when they started.

Sarah couldn't remain seated; she needed to verify if her name was on the list. Departmental heads were trying to negotiate the list's contents before its official release. Some had their favorites on the list, while others were relieved to see some names of colleagues gone.

After prolonged discussions, the head manager stood firm in his decision for those listed to leave the company, citing various reasons. The more they debated, the more resolute he became in enforcing the company's decision. This caused anxiety among some managers who were now at risk.

Once the meeting concluded, the list was posted on the notice board. Sarah quickly rushed over to read for herself the names affected by the workforce reduction.

She was particularly intrigued by the bolded, red-highlighted portion at the end.

"All national service personnel will be required to leave the mining site at the end of their service period. No one will be retained. Apply through the company website and await further instructions," the notice announced.

"So, that man wasn't joking with me" she said bewildered, standing with both hands on her waist.

"Where will I go after my national service if I'm not retained? Should I call Raymond? Or should I meet with the man who offered to help?" Sarah pondered to herself.

"I'll need to meet with him this evening before my national service becomes a laughingstock. Let me review the list again," she decided and walked closer to the notice board.

"I'm sure Sarah is in complete shock. She's been standing there for more than twenty minutes. Now we're in the same boat," a colleague taunted from a distance.

"We warned her, but she wouldn't listen. She needs to mend this wound before it's exposed to a torrent of laughter," another person chimed in, laughing.

"Almost everyone who assured me is on this list. And of all people, Fred, who helped me get this job, is not on the list" Sarah queried still standing at the notice board.

"Does he have shares in the company? Or is he hiding his true self from me?" she muttered as she walked confidently to her office.

Upon seeing her, her friends burst into laughter, then fell silent. Once she was out of earshot, they continued laughing, and everyone returned to their tasks. Sarah was annoyed by their behavior but continued speaking to herself.

"I won't let failure define me," she muttered, picking up her bag.

"Tell our supervisor I'm not feeling well, so I'll be back to work on Monday," she instructed.

"Who?" they all asked in unison.

It surprised Sarah that they all spoke at once. It seemed that none of them wanted to convey the message to the supervisor. The room fell silent for a moment.

"I'll tell Mr. Nyarko when he arrives. Get well soon," a colleague said with a smile to break the silence.

"Thank you very much, my friend. Please let him know that my stomach is hurting, and I left my hospital card at home that's why I'm seeking medical treatment elsewhere. May God bless you abundantly," Sarah responded before leaving.

"But who says I will inform our supervisor about her leaving work? Does she think she can fool any of us? I'm too old for her comic behavior. Well, if anyone will tell Mr. Nyarko, then the person can do that," a cute girl sitting with them said after Sarah had left.

"Why did you admit to informing our supervisor, knowing perfectly well you wouldn't? I know we don't like her, but you must keep to your promise," a guy said in an angry tone.

"What promise? Even the leaders of our country can't keep to their little promises. How much more me?" the cute girl explained with a frowned face.

"From the look of things, I never promised. You can also tell him. I only said that so she will know we like her but not to be her slave, running errands for her," she added getting the attention of her colleagues.

Sarah had left the security post. She flagged down a taxi and got in. She was still unhappy about the management's decision. The taxi driver noticed her mood but didn't know how to start a conversation. Her expression was glum, and she seemed to have forgotten her destination.

The car seemed a little new, and the interior design looked exquisite. The hip pop music rocked louder, and the driver nodded his head as he accelerated. He wondered why Sarah sat in the car tight-lipped.

"Please put on the seatbelt" the driver instructed while he turned down the volume of the radio.

"Where are you headed, miss?" the driver asked, trying to gloat Sarah.

"I'm going to..." she paused, then handed the driver an address and fastened her seatbelt.

"Alright, it'll be fifty cedis. I've lowered the fare because of your beauty," the driver added and horned at a motor rider who sped past his car.

"Fifty cedis?" Sarah burst out.

"When did the fare become so high?" she yawped seeming aghast.

"Are you charging me more because of my dress? I'm a national service person, and our allowances haven't been paid for the last six months," she lied.

"But your company should pay you, not the government. I know your allowances have been reflecting in your account for over four months. Please don't try to deceive me" the taxi driver debunked, turning the radio off.

"After my national service, I sent letters to every ministry and agency, but I received no response," he tried explaining, pressing on the brake pedal of the car to stop when the traffic light had turned red.

"I'm doing 'work and pay' with this taxi so I can feed myself. I hope to own this car after five years of paying off the debt. Nowhere is easy, ma'am. So, please understand the fare. We're almost there," he explained.

"I only have thirty cedis on me. I'm meeting someone at this hotel. We can go there, and I'll get your balance for you. Please don't cause a scene; I'm going through a lot, and I have a terrible headache," Sarah mumbled after checking her purse.

"I'm not a bad guy, ma'am. I hold a master's degree in procurement. The economy is pushing good people to do desperate things because of hunger" the taxi driver said and turned the steering wheel of the car to the left.

"This is the hotel. It's one of the top-classes in the area. Whoever you're meeting must be quite wealthy," the driver explained as he turned off the car's engine.

"Why are you dropping me off here? Why not go inside the gates?" Sarah asked, looking clutched.

"The sign on the wall says taxis aren't allowed in. I can't deal with a lot of protocols just to waste time" the taxi driver said, pointing to the signpost.

"Besides, it's only fifty cedis you're paying. Let's go so you can get my money and I can get back to work" he added fazed.

Sarah wasn't comfortable crossing the street and walking a distance to reach the hotel entrance. Her phone beeped, indicating a message. She checked it;

it was the hotel room number. Feeling a bit dizzy, she pushed herself to go; she needed to find something to eat.

The taxi driver was waiting outside, urging her to leave the car and head to the hotel. She pulled out her phone and saw messages from Mr. Nyarko, which she chose to ignore. With a heavy heart, she got out of the car.

"Ma'am, watch out for the oncoming cars... OH MY GOD!!!" the taxi driver shouted.

A car hit Sarah, sending her tumbling into the middle of the road before speeding away. The taxi driver rushed to her side, while others gathered to assist. They helped him lift her into the taxi and sped off to the hospital. The taxi driver used his siren to navigate the heavy traffic, making his way to the hospital quickly.

Nurses rushed to the scene to provide immediate care. The taxi driver handled all the necessary paperwork and carried Sarah's bag, hoping to find a contact number or health insurance card. He found a company card in her bag, which was a stroke of luck.

Meanwhile, Raymond had concluded a meeting with business executives interested in investing in the company. His presentation had been spot-on, and they agreed to invest. The management was thrilled with his outstanding performance.

"Could you excuse us for a moment?" the CEO asked Raymond.

"In just one meeting, Raymond had made us five times richer. He's been with this company for years, and he's truly exceptional. I think we should surprise him with a trip to Dubai," the CEO whispered to the entire management.

"I'm on board with that idea. He works tirelessly and doesn't even take his annual leave, not even for a week," another person added.

"I agree wholeheartedly. Let's make it a trip for two since he's dating Rita. He'd probably want to go with her," the secretary suggested.

"Yes, I support this idea. Let's take a vote and initiate the visa application process. It'll be a month-long vacation, all expenses covered by the company. Secretary, please send him an email outlining all the details once the plans are finalized," the CEO concluded before ending the meeting.

"Hello, are you Raymond?" the taxi driver asked over the phone.

"Yes, I am. Who's calling?" Raymond responded.

"Could you please send me the fifty cedis you owe me? I was expecting you to give it to me after the lady you intended to meet crossed the road" the taxi driver paused and continued when Raymond didn't respond.

"She said you'd give me the fare when we reached your hotel room. But before she could finish crossing, there was a loud noise..." the taxi driver explained walking out of the emergency unit.

"Is this Mr. Ameyaw? Are you trying to scam me for money? Don't think you can fool me with a different number. I recognize your voice from how you speak. You didn't say 'oh,' but I still recognize you," Raymond said, heaving a sigh at his office.

"Please, I'm not Mr. Ameyaw. I found your card in the bag of a passenger I picked up from a mining company. Her name is Sarah. I am the taxi driver who took her to the hospital" he explained.

"A car hit her, and I don't even know if she's alive. Please send me the money so I can leave the hospital. I need to work; otherwise, I'll go to bed hungry tonight" he added.

"Sarah? Which hospital? Send me the GPS coordinates," Raymond requested and promptly ended the call.

Charles, the taxi driver sent the coordinates to Raymond through a text message as soon as the call ended.

Raymond was enroute, guided by the GPS coordinates. Unfortunately, he lost his way. He tried calling the taxi driver multiple times, but there was no answer. He dialed Sarah's number, but it was switched off.

"What's going on? Should I just head home and meet Rita for our date?" Raymond questioned, looking confused.

"Is Sarah trying to deceive me along with the taxi driver?" he wondered aloud, checking the time.

"Where are you?" Charles called back.

"I'm on my way, but…"

"Then why were you calling me? I came outside to find you, but I didn't see any driver approaching. Are you really coming?" Charles retorted in an angry tone.

"You're seriously delaying me, and you'll pay triple when you finally arrive," he continued, still angry.

"I was calling to ask for directions; I'm lost. But you should have at least answered to hear me out," Raymond replied politely.

Back at the office, Mr. Nyarko arrived and inquired about Sarah, but nobody knew where she was. He was genuinely upset that she had left without any notice. The human resource manager was conducting a head count of the national service personnel and Sarah's presence was much needed. He tried calling Sarah multiple times, but her phone was out of reach. He returned to her colleagues, asking if they had an alternate number for her. They all replied in the negative.

"What do I do now? If I don't have a good explanation for the manager during the inspection, I might lose my job," Mr. Nyarko lamented.

The manager conducted the head count and asked questions about what the service personnel had learned so far. A particularly articulate and bright girl provided thorough answers, impressing the manager.

"Where is Sarah? Is she not in this department?" the manager asked while examining the list.

The colleagues exchanged glances but remained silent. The manager went to Mr. Nyarko's office to inquire about Sarah's whereabouts. Just as he turned, Mr. Nyarko entered.

"Sarah has applied to terminate her service. She's moved out," Mr. Nyarko reported.

"Did she mention why she made that decision?" the manager inquired.

"She says she received a job interview invitation from another company, and she might get employed there, sir," he responded.

Sarah's colleagues were surprised to hear this from Mr. Nyarko. They knew why she wasn't at work, but hearing those reasons from their supervisor left them pondering. After a brief moment of silence and exchanged looks, they resumed their work.

"Looks like Sarah's opportunity had slipped away. You're articulate and clever. What's your name?" the manager asked, turning to the cute girl in the office.

"Me?" she turned around, somewhat surprised.

"Yes, you, my dear. You're exceptionally bright, and your supervisor has spoken highly of you," he responded.

"My name is Issabella Ansah," she replied, taken aback.

"Meet me at the office on Monday. Bring along your certificates and identification cards," the manager instructed and walked back to the supervisor's office.

Issabella was stunned; she hadn't anticipated such a turn of events. It was a mix of emotions she couldn't fully comprehend. Countless questions raced through her mind.

"People were just let go from the company, and yet she's being offered a job. What's going on?" a colleague speculated.

"I apologize, but we can't hire everyone. Regardless of the situation, always strive for excellence. I know many people have been manipulated by those who claim to be managers here. This wound they've caused will be hard to heal, as management isn't keen on hiring at the moment," the manager advised after returning to the office of the personnel and picked up his phone which he had left behind.

6

It is indeed true that life is more precious than gold. However, situations compel people to trample on souls to alleviate their predicament.

"See, on your complimentary card, aren't you the manager of that big company? So why then don't you know your way around this place?" Charles asked surprised, walking towards the hospital's main gate.

"Instead of employing people like us in your company, you employ ladies who know nothing. Look at what you caused to such a delightful girl, all in the name of 'meet me at the hotel'" he added, throwing his hands in the air as he walked past the security man.

"Take the next turn on your left or right from where you have reached. Aren't you using the GPS address I sent you?" Charles yelled.

Raymond was truly angry about how the taxi driver was talking to him, so he hanged up the call and followed his direction. Charles was also angry that Raymond was delaying. Many of his customers called him, but he couldn't answer any because of the situation he found himself.

"The only thing some managers know is to take advantage of young girls. You meet a delicate girl you want to marry, and she is not a virgin. All in the name of a manager who gave her a job in return for sexual pleasure. I don't always blame the ladies who fall victim to this. Our country is in serious hardship," Charles said to himself, clearly irritated.

"My brother, what you are saying is true. My biggest problem is that the work these ladies get is not even a permanent job. You can only keep the job when you constantly have affairs with these managers. They are not true to their words and ruin the future of our young ladies. I pity our ladies a lot, and I wish they could understand the situation. I hope they could realize this in time," a man interrupted upon hearing Charles's fume.

"It's very sad our country has no regard for university certificates. I only wish they would sell the country and give us our share," Charles said.

"My brother, even if they share, a graduate like me working as a diener won't get a cedi. Our country is awfully difficult, but I believe patience is the key, and at the right time, God will open the heavenly doors of riches and success. Anyway, my name is Philip" he added.

"You work as a diener?" Charles shouted.

"Then I need to thank God for being a taxi driver. I don't think I can risk myself for this job. I'm also Charles" he added with a sense of relief.

"Did you apply for it, or was your father a diener, and he secured the position for you as other managers have been doing?" Charles asked, surprised.

"Hmm… my brother, I actually applied for this job, and I followed up every day to know the status of my application" Philip said as if he was ready to cry.

"I would be happy to drive a taxi, but I don't have the money to buy a car" he dolefully added cleaning the sweat on his face.

"You are mocking me because of my job. Similarly, a manager will mock you for driving a taxi. We are not in a perfect world, but soon, things will improve" he cinched, now having his hands on his waist.

"Working here is not my joy, but as long as I can feed myself and remain honest, it's enough. I believe this isn't my permanent place. God is preparing me for better things," he established, with his face now lit with hope.

"Then, Philip, you are very brave to work as a mortuary attendant" Charles tantalized.

"I don't even think I can move an inch close to the door. Do you bathe them?" he asked startled, with both hands stiffed on his stomach.

"My brother, working here has taught me a lot about life. I asked so many questions just as you are doing now. I perfectly understand your doubts and fears. When someone dies, it's absolutely the end of their lives" Philip lamented.

"They have no place to go, and they remain like that until the resurrection day. Both the ugly and the beautiful, the rich and the poor, the president, and the cleaner, are laid to rest in the ground. The pride we carry around ends as soon as we die," he said and sighed.

"But I know when someone dies, you must be careful with them because they can harm you. Some will even turn into ghosts to haunt you. I'm much afraid of the dead," Charles said, trembling.

"There is absolutely no life after death. Most times, our thoughts haunt us to imagine these ghosts. You must work with a clean heart the same way you live your life. Prayers should always be your shield and guard" Philip said confidently.

"I'm not afraid of my job, and I do it with passion because that's where I find myself now. When God opens the door of grace for me to work elsewhere, I would gladly go. What I believe is that in life, you must start from somewhere" he advised.

"Just understand that there is no power in the dead; that's why you must serve God, love, pray, and forgive others now that you have breath. During the resurrection hour, the dead in Christ shall rise and meet God in heaven," he explained and paused.

"You've given me much education, and I appreciate it a lot. I would come for more insight about the dead. Now that I have life, I will do my possible best to touch lives and do the will of God," Charles said and looked around to see if Raymond had arrived.

"I'm glad you understand the work I do and the importance of the living to the dead. As soon as you die, you become worthless. Even families, after a week or two, forget that you once existed and start living their normal lives" Philip pointed out after a nurse walked briskly behind them.

"I will urge you to worship your God in truth and in spirit, but if you don't attend church, I will urge you to find a good one and attend. God bless you. The siren you are hearing signals the death of someone. I need to go and assist," he said and patted Charles' left shoulder and began to walk away.

"So how many people die in a day?" Charles asked in dismay.

"More than you can imagine," he shouted in a distance as he walked quickly to the mortuary.

Charles received a call, and it was Raymond. This time, he picked up after the second ring. He went to meet him and narrated everything to him. Raymond also explained the reason for his coming and made him aware they were old friends, and he didn't call her to the hotel.

It was ridiculously hard for Charles to believe, but he had no option. He was waiting to hear Raymond talk about the transportation fare, but he didn't.

"Please, my money" Charles yelled when he saw Raymond walking away.

"How much is it?"

"It's one hundred and eighty cedis only."

"Show me to her room, and I will pay when we return."

"But, sir, how do you break me? I've been here for the past four hours waiting for you to come and pay me. You came from your car; you want me to escort you to her sick bed? Do you take me for a fool or what? Can you pay my waiting fee?" Charles said angrily.

"I need to be sure she is really at the hospital. What if it's a prank? This country is very unpredictable, and people arc capable of anything. Will you show me?" Raymond replied but in a calmer tone, while they stood at the entrance of the emergency unit.

They walked a distance from the emergency room to the female ward…

"Yes, now you've shown me the ward, but to make everything complete and get your money, you need to finish this journey. Both of us should enter. What if there is a bomb in the room?" Raymond said pointing to the door.

"Bomb at the hospital? On a hospital bed? Hmm… I can't believe this" Charles asked surprised.

"I'm afraid of blood, and I can't watch her again. I still have the accident scene in my memory, so please enter. You can have my car keys." Charles was at his wit's end.

"Car keys are not enough. Come with me," Raymond instructed and walked closer to the door.

"Oh, my God! It's Sarah. She is brutally injured" Raymond exclaimed upon setting eyes on Sarah the moment he entered the ward.

"Who hit a beautiful girl like this and ran away? Some people are heartless. Aaaw… Sarah, I told you to stay with me, but you never listened," Raymond began crying while trying to hold Sarah's injured left arm.

"Boss, can you give me my two hundred cedis?" Charles said as he walked towards him.

Raymond dipped his hand into his left pocket and gave him one hundred cedis notes. Charles counted it twice to be sure the amount was exactly what he requested. A smile gashed all over his face.

"Should I wait further? He is extraordinarily rich, and I'm sure he won't mind giving me more," he thought to himself.

"I'm not sure Raymond is in the office" Rita thought to herself and ordered a ride.

"If he was, he would have finished the meeting by now" she added as she stood up from the middle of the couch where she had been sitting for the past thirty minutes, watching her favorite telenovela.

"Let me meet him there so he won't have any excuse for being tired. I can't miss this date. It's going to be my second time going there," Rita said to herself with a smile, grabbed her handbag, and left the house when the driver arrived.

Rita was halfway to Raymond's office and yet none of his numbers went through after she called. She was worried because it was getting late and couldn't understand why his phone was off.

"Madam, it's best you visit the office to see for yourself what's happening. Contemplating and thinking will not give you the answers you need. Please seek, and you shall find," the taxi driver said after navigating a curve.

Instantly, a call came through Rita's phone.

"You are right. Let me speak with Mr. Ameyaw. He can give me the necessary information I need. I don't trust guys, especially the handsome ones. He could be in another woman's arms and tell you he is busy with a presentation," Rita consented with the driver and rejected the call.

Rita rescinded her decision to call Mr. Ameyaw since they were then close to the office.

"Madam Rita ooh, how are you? What are you doing here at this time of the night without Raymond, my boss?" Mr. Ameyaw asked.

"I received a message from Raymond concerning a late meeting he was having. However, we planned a date, and I decided to meet him here, so he won't complain about being tired after the meeting. The lights in the office are off, and he is not picking up my calls. I can't see his car in the parking lot." Rita explained looking a bit worried.

"Meeting?   Parents-Teachers'   Association meeting?"

"Mr. Ameyaw, please be serious for once" Rita fumed.

"We are talking about matters of the heart. I asked, didn't you have any meeting here?" she added chomp at the bit.

"Oh, meeting! There was! I even went to buy the drinks and water. Sometimes you need to be patient with me. I'm aging, and I forget things easily. Your darling husband is now the star of the company. He won the contract again, and everyone was happy.

I'm the only sad person," he said hoping to calm her down.

"Why are you sad?" Rita asked concerned.

"All the contracts and fat money the company receives, it has nothing to do with our salaries. My salary has been jogging for the past eight years. No allowance nor bonuses," he explained.

"Get this money for something. I need to go home. It's getting too late, and the driver is honking as if I'm running away with his money," Rita said and gave him fifty cedis.

"Don't go home. I'm very sure he is waiting for you at the dating spot. You know my boss can be full of surprises. Just pass by and see if he is around or not," Mr. Ameyaw advised.

Rita turned her phone to silent mode when she noticed Mr. Ameyaw had seen her ignoring calls from Paul. She walked to the car and picked up the call. The driver was terribly angry for being delayed for quite some time.

"Paul, why are you disturbing me at this ungodly hour?" Rita shouted after finally picking the call.

7

We are faced with the decision of playing it safe, being apprehensive about potential negative outcomes, or taking risks and living a life that truly resonates with our hearts. While life chooses our acquaintances, it is ultimately up to us to choose the people we want to surround ourselves with and call our friends.

Isabella was restless in her bed, pondering the miraculous turn her life had taken. She had never expected to be retained by the mining company, but fate, working in mysterious ways, had granted her that favor. It felt like a dream to her, and she struggled to express the overwhelming joy within her.

"What will my friends think of me? Are they speculating whether I have a connection with the human resource manager? Are they gossiping about me, or genuinely happy for my success?" she questioned herself, grappling with a flurry of thoughts.

"I should approach them and assure them that, should any opportunity arise, I'll help them find connections. But is that the right thing to do?" she contemplated, rolling on the bed from left to right in her cute lingerie.

"I'm afraid these guys might feel hurt. Securing a job is a sensitive matter, and I need to ensure I give my best regardless of any whispers behind my back," she reassured herself before retiring to bed.

Raymond found himself stuck in heavy traffic-jam, the cars were heavily lined up and it was a snail-pace traffic-jam. He appeared visibly agitated. As he sat in the gloom of his frustration, thoughts about Rita flashed through his mind. He wondered why Rita hadn't contacted him again; he thought about Charles, then he started thinking about the traffic-jam. It was like a procession of black ants displaying around dry dead leaves looking for food. He glanced at his watch; it read 10 p.m. He realized it was Friday and a plan began to form in his mind.

A song played softly in the silence of his car. Now, the traffic-jam started to ease, and Raymond heaved a sigh of relief. He got to the supermarket and saw many beautiful teddy bears, but he was careful because he knew Rita's favorite color. He spotted a pink-colored teddy bear and immediately knew she would love it. He then moved to the cashier after grabbing two chocolate bars. As he walked out of the supermarket, he whistled a tune from the hymn book. He was still very excited even as he pulled out of the parking lot; he was going to surprise Rita and some kind of ecstasy overflowed his heart as he drove.

"This evening is going to be a romantic one. I can hardly wait to surprise her" he fantasised.

"My love, I hope I'm not interrupting. I still love you deeply and desire a chance to mend our relationship. I acknowledge the pain I've caused you, but trust me, I've undergone a transformation. I've committed to attending church, quitting drinking and promiscuity. Please grant me another chance, and I pledge to make better choices," Paul pleaded over the phone.

"Another chance? How many chances have I given you? More than I can count, yet none proved worthy of your deplorable behavior. I invested in this relationship, but you disrespected me by engaging with women beneath my dignity, all under the guise of me not meeting your desires," Rita retorted.

"But what I mean is..."

"Don't say anything, Paul. I am now dating someone who treats me with respect and love. We are in a committed relationship, and I will not jeopardize it for you. Please, unless you have something important to discuss, I need to make an important call," Rita concluded and ended the call abruptly.

"Who??? Raym..." the call was disconnected.

"Driver, take me to the Sea Hotel. It's just a two-minutes' drive followed by a ten-minutes' walk from here" Rita said in animosity, directing the driver.

"I visited there with Paul once, and those memories are still vivid. He is a good person," Rita contemplated aloud, turning off the display of her phone.

"The same Paul you were talking to a few minutes ago?" the taxi driver asked, surprised.

"Yes, that's him!"

"Do you still have feelings for him?" the taxi driver inquired as he drove.

"No, it's not that" Rita quickly answered.

"At least you should have a serious conversation with him to explain your reasons," the taxi driver advised while turning into the hotel's entrance.

"Everything that needed explanation was said. He even pressured me relentlessly, but I stood my ground. I recognized his addiction to sex and his willingness to go to any extent, even paying for it. I caught him numerous times, and out of love, I forgave him, understanding that people make mistakes and deserve forgiveness."

"Praise the Lord!" the taxi driver exclaimed as he turned off the car's engine.

"Could you stay with me as I wait for my fiancé? I've looked everywhere, and he's nowhere to be found. Let's wait for fifteen more minutes. If he doesn't show up, I'll give him a call," Rita suggested, and they both settled in.

"I empathize with your feelings, madam. Do you still have residual affection for Paul?" the driver probed.

"I don't believe we can rekindle our relationship. He truly is a good person, I admit, but his actions have left indelible scars. They resurface every time I hear his name. He may care, but that alone doesn't build a solid foundation for a relationship. Responsibility is a cornerstone of happiness for a woman," Rita explained.

At the hospital, Charles alerted a nurse to witness Sarah's behavior. Sarah was moving her head and murmuring words to herself. The nurse promptly fetched the doctor, who examined Sarah and studied her medical chart. Afterward, the doctor jotted down notes in her file.

"Please ensure she receives these medications. They will help calm her down and grant her a restful sleep for about five hours, enhancing her recovery," the doctor instructed the nurse, who noted down the prescription and left to retrieve the drugs.

"Mr. Charles, kindly acquire these medications for Sarah as per the doctor's orders," the nurse wrote the prescriptions and handed them to Charles.

"Auntie nurse, she has active National Health Insurance, as indicated in her purse" Charles softly said as he showed the card to the nurse.

"These medications are not covered by the health insurance, I'm afraid," the nurse clarified.

"When does anything get covered at hospitals? What exactly does health insurance cover? Even a simple drug to induce sleep isn't covered?" Charles said almost raising his voice.

"I shudder to think what might occur if the situation were more dire," he lamented.

"I don't manage accounts here. My responsibility is my patients' well-being. Please expedite the medication procurement before she injures herself again," the nurse replied and departed.

"What sort of country is this? Nothing comes without a cost. Even cotton wool isn't covered by health insurance" he said throwing his hands in the air.

"I should call Raymond and ask him to send funds for the medication and fuel. Hosting a lady in a hotel seems to drain your resources," Charles muttered, dialing Raymond's number.

Meanwhile, Rita and the taxi driver engaged in a deep conversation about Paul under the lovers bench close to the pool side. The taxi driver was making an effort to persuade her to reconsider her decision regarding Paul. She countered with various instances and circumstances that rendered their relationship untenable. As she glanced at her watch, she realized she had two minutes left to call Raymond.

"Please try to overlook his past transgressions. I believe the positive aspects outweigh the negative ones. A second chance may not be far-fetched," the taxi driver offered, and a hand suddenly covered Rita's face.

"Who's there? Raymond, this isn't funny," Rita exclaimed, her face still covered by the hand.

The person remained silent, leaving the taxi driver perplexed by the situation.

"The perfume is unusual, but Raymond, enough! My eyes hurt. You know I dislike such pranks. Don't spoil this lovely evening" Rita said trying hard to push the hands off her face.

The person signaled the taxi driver to remain silent as Rita sought a description. The person leaned in, allowing Rita to feel his breathe near her ear.

"Raymond, this is getting unsettling. This joke could backfire on us. Please stop," Rita implored.

And then, with her eyes still covered, she whispered, "You're scaring me, Raymond. This could be costly. I don't like these games."

The person finally removed his hand from Rita's face, revealing himself to be Paul. Rita cast a glance at Paul and then at the taxi driver; she was confused.

"Do you two know each other?" Rita inquired.

"Who?" both responded.

"I mean, Paul, do you know this taxi driver?" Rita directed the question to Paul.

"No, I don't know him. Do you recognize me?" Paul answered and asked.

At this time the taxi driver was quiet and speechless.

"No, I don't recall meeting you anywhere. Madam, I need to leave since your visitor is here." The taxi driver said, ignoring the confusion on Rita's face.

"It will cost you eighty cedis" he added looking at Paul's face.

"Keep the change" Paul said, paying the taxi driver with a fresh one hundred cedis note from his wallet.

The taxi driver took the fresh note with excitement, looked at it, and smelled it. The notes had a distinct fresh smell. He raised it towards the light to check if it was a genuine note. As Rita and Paul walked away from the pool side towards the club, the taxi driver sped off through the street in-front-of the club house.

Rita looked with fury into Paul's face and begun to question him.

"Do you make a habit of following all the women you've been with?" she paused and looked outside.

"Is this your approach, trailing them from one place to another?" she sat back on her seat looking straight into Paul's eyes, waiting for answers.

Paul looked embarrassed. He felt like a child. It was not his intention to follow Rita. It was only a coincidence. At this time Rita was being rude. Her tone was not pleasant.

"What are you doing here? Why were you following me?" Rita questioned; her gaze locked on Paul.

Paul, realizing he'd spent over twenty minutes waiting and that Raymond was a no-show, began to explain.

Paul signalled the server and ordered some drinks and meat. He requested the DJ to play romantic songs.

"I'm not chasing after women, rather someone my heart longs to be with" Paul looked straight into Rita's eyes while attempting to go on his knees.

"Rita, I love you. I deeply regret the pain I caused you. Please remember the good times and the beautiful memories we've had" Paul held on to Rita's hands while kneeling on one knee and spoke calmly.

"Remember this place? We sat over there and spoke at length. That was when we shared our first kiss" he explained, pointing to a wooden chair under the summer hut.

"Paul, I'm currently in a serious relationship, planning for marriage. My fiancé will be coming for the dowry negotiations next Thursday. It's too late for a reconciliation," she explained.

"Do you love him? Look into my eyes and tell me," Paul urged.

Raymond answered Charles' call, sending him money for both the medication and fuel. Eager to receive more money, Charles provided a figure without confirming it with the pharmacy. Excited about the low cost of a sleeping pill, he headed to a gas station for fuel and then proceeded to the pharmacy.

"Good morning... I mean, good evening. How are you doing?" he handed the prescription form to the lovely lady.

"Good evening, I'm doing well, and yourself?" the medicine counter assistant responded, entering the medication name on her laptop.

"The cost of the medication is two hundred and fifty cedis," she informed.

"Two hundred and fifty? How much is the sleeping pill?" he asked, surprised.

"The sleeping pill is only one hundred and eighty cedis; the difference is for the other medications," the lady clarified.

"A pill that just induces sleep costs that much?" Charles asked looking both surprised and confused.

"I wonder what the price of a death pill would be!" he added, trying to control his anger.

"What kind of world are we creating? No jobs, no money... nothing. When you steal, it's a jobless graduate who will beat you to death. Can we survive in this world? I pray God intervenes soon," Charles lamented.

"Since we're in this country, you must understand the system and adapt. Serve God faithfully and pray for Heaven. There's no perfect place, my brother. The best place is where you find yourself," she empathised.

"But can a war between two countries affect the entire world? If certain countries engage in a war, are we all supposed to line up and surrender to death?" he asked raising his two hands in the air.

"The escalating prices of goods are a major concern too" she added unexpectedly.

"I thought healthcare centers would be exceptional. I even fear they'll double this price by morning if I don't purchase it now" he giggled with his left hand on his waist and right hand on the medicine counter.

"Gradually, people won't be able to afford healthcare, and our population will decline. But we can make a difference for our country, the two of us," Charles said, gazing into her eyes with a smile.

"We? Save the world? How?" the medicine counter assistant asked, astonished.

"Let me tell you how we can save the world. Write your number on the prescription form, and I'll call you tomorrow. I need to get back to the hospital before things worsen," Charles told her.

She took the paper and jotted down her number where Charles indicated. The girl was indeed beautiful, almost breathtaking.

"Please use the medicine responsibly, not to manipulate any lady," she advised, both sharing a smile.

"If I were to use it on anyone, it would be you. What beauty!" Charles murmured to himself as he left the pharmacy.

Charles had already returned to the hospital, finding Sarah calmer. Seeing him, she offered a gracious smile. A nurse promptly administered the drugs to her.

"You should head home. She'll be stronger when she wakes up" the nurse said to Charles when she saw he was dozing on the chair beside Sarah's bed.

"Prepare some light soup for her in the morning," the nurse told another patient's relative who sat closer to Sarah's bed.

Charles turned around, checking if the advice was directed at him. He had no cooking skills, especially when it came to estimating the right amount of salt.

"Sure, I'll get it done first thing tomorrow morning" he said to himself, winked and walked out of the ward without confirming from the nurse.

As Charles drove home, he laughed at the idea of cooking and then decided to call Raymond for assistance. On getting home, he dropped his car keys on a small table near his mattress, removed his clothes and just before he entered the bathroom, a call came through.

"Hey, are you still at the hospital?" Raymond inquired.

"No, sir. I just got back to my room, about to take a shower and sleep. I've been trying to reach you with some updates from the nurses," Charles responded.

"Updates? How's Sarah? Do they need more money?" Raymond asked, concerned.

"Updates, yes! Sarah is doing well, and the medications I got are working as expected. They might need more funds since the health insurance doesn't cover any medicines," Charles explained.

"What's the matter then?" Raymond wondered.

"The nurse with a limp instructed us to prepare a light soup for Sarah for tomorrow, for her breakfast," Charles explained.

"That's no problem. I'll buy it from a restaurant, as I won't have time to prepare it. I wanted to check up on Sarah, but since you're back home, I'll visit tomorrow. We have something to discuss tomorrow. Please remind me," Raymond said before ending the call.

"A discussion with me tomorrow? I hope it's not about interrogating me regarding Sarah. God, please let this conversation be a turning point in my life," Charles sighed before entering the bathroom.

Raymond had ignored five calls from Mr. Ameyaw. Mr. Ameyaw sent a message to Raymond explaining the situation with Rita, but he couldn't read it immediately as he was engaged with the Sea hotel's security personnel.

"Please turn left and drive straight. And do axle parking," the security guard instructed Raymond, leading the way.

Due to the congested parking area, the security guard directed him to a spot where Rita wouldn't notice his car. Raymond spotted Rita with a man but found it hard to believe it was her. He decided to confirm by dialing her number. After ignoring numerous calls, Rita responded with a message after the tenth attempt. He couldn't believe what he saw afterwards. From where he stood, he could see Rita sharing a kiss with an unknown guy. It was as if an elephant had been put on his chest. He felt so heartbroken and walked into his car. He remained in the car with his head bowed down and had both hands on the steering wheel. After about 10 minutes of agony, he drove off.

"Rita, please, I'm eager to hear what you have to say. I'm willing to do anything for you." Paul said softly still holding on tight to Rita's hands.

"Waitress, please bring more drinks and goat meat," Paul requested.

As the server approached with a variety of drinks, she smiled and even winked at Paul. Rita didn't notice because she was engrossed in checking her phone.

"Please select your drink. The goat meat will be ready in five minutes," the server added after Paul made his choice.

"I'm actually quite full. Please package the remaining drinks. It's getting late, and we need to leave," Rita declined, still focused on her phone.

"Please prepare our bill" Paul quickly told the server and stood up.

"I'll give you another chance but remember that I'm currently with Raymond. Please don't overwhelm me with calls and messages. I'll respond and call you when I'm comfortable. Also, I'd like you to transfer five thousand cedis to my account. I plan to start a business," Rita shared her conditions.

"I'll transfer the money to your account first thing tomorrow morning. But how long will you be with Raymond? When can I hope to have you for myself?" he inquired.

"I'm not sure exactly when, but I believe it will happen sooner than you can imagine. I'm watching you closely. If you make even a small mistake, don't come begging for my forgiveness. If you truly love me, steer clear off these young girls and remember my earlier words," Rita stated firmly, rising from her seat.

Paul settled the bills and accompanied Rita to her home. They engaged in light conversation by her gate for a while and exchanged hugs.

Raymond had returned home and was lying in bed, attempting to forget the events at the hotel. However, all his efforts were in vain. He grabbed his phone, scrolling through the pictures he had taken. He couldn't believe that a seemingly good Christian lady would betray him, even going as far as engaging in public kisses. He deleted some blurry pictures and edited the clearer ones.

Opening WhatsApp, he navigated to Rita's chat and selected some of the pictures to send to her. Yet, he hesitated and eventually deleted the pictures from her chat. Checking her "last seen" status, he noticed she was online.

8

"Some people and things are difficult for us to leave behind and release. Nevertheless, it's crucial to remember that letting go doesn't signify the end of everything; instead, it marks the beginning of a new chapter in life."

It was morning, and the weather felt a bit chilly. The wind roared as if rain was imminent, but the clear and colorful clouds provided no indication. The atmosphere was charged with tension as many hurried to their jobs, and drivers showed little consideration for school children and their parents attempting to cross the road. The voices of traders enthusiastically promoting their goods resonated loudly. Hawkers selling an array of products lined the road, striving to make a living.

Raymond had woken up late and was trying his best to prepare quickly and leave for work. Just when he had finished brushing his teeth, a call came through. He was first hesitant to pick but eventually did.

"Are you Raymond? Please come to the hospital immediately," a nurse said on the phone.

"But Charles told me he used his details for everything. How did the nurse get my number?" Raymond questioned, grappling with the numerous queries.

"It sounds urgent. I need to hurry, especially with the food, before something bad happens to Sarah," he hastily dressed and left his house without taking a shower.

In a matter of minutes, Raymond arrived at the hospital with a bowl of food. He spotted Charles waiting at the entrance, and Charles explained the urgency of the situation, as he had received a call from the nurse as well. They both wondered why they were summoned.

"Is this the soup the nurse requested?" Charles inquired.

"Yes. Did the nurse call me because of the food?" Raymond asked looking worried.

"I don't think so, but it might be a factor," Charles speculated.

As they approached Sarah's room, Charles pointed out the nurse who had called him. Raymond was anxious to know why his presence was urgently required, so he approached the nurse for an explanation.

"Madam Nurse, I'm the one you called, asking me to come to the hospital immediately. What's wrong with Sarah? Is there a problem?" Raymond inquired urgently.

"Alright, you're Raymond? A young man who was beside Sarah's bed asked me to call you. He instructed me to sound serious and demand your immediate attention at the hospital. He even suggested I tell you that Sarah was in critical condition, but I explained the implications of such a lie," the nurse explained.

"So, there's nothing wrong with Sarah, and Charles asked you to call me with such urgency, and you did?" Raymond questioned looking disappointed.

"Yes, because he said you were bringing medicine for Sarah, and the doctor needed it early in the morning," she confirmed seemingly confused.

"Medicine? He only asked me to buy fufu and light soup with hot pepper for Sarah. I even ground the pepper myself because the cooks were busy. I gave him money to buy those medicines yesterday, so I know nothing about medicine," he clarified, showing her the bowl.

"The medication wasn't available, so the doctor left without attending to Sarah. She needs to take the medicine now, or she might experience severe complications within the next four hours. As for the food, I'm certain that was his request. The doctor has advised against giving her water, let alone fufu," the nurse explained, visibly concerned.

Raymond turned and noticed Charles walking towards them. Charles seemed unperturbed and unaware of Sarah's condition if she didn't receive the necessary medication.

"Charles, come over here!" the nurse called out to him.

"Is this food for Sarah or for yourself?" Raymond asked Charles, who seemed stunned.

Fred had reached his workplace and was inquiring about Sarah's whereabouts. However, none of her colleagues knew where she was. He consulted his friends, who had shown interest in her romantically, and they all shared their thoughts.

"Fred, why are you so concerned about a grown woman? She might be in a man's room. Never place your trust in women, especially these service personnel. They can break your heart without a second thought," one of his friends commented.

"I've known Sarah for a while, and she rarely visits anyone" Fred said looking in the direction of his friend.

"The only friend I know she has is her work. She is cautious about who she spends time with. To be missing for more than a day is unusual. She is friendly but careful about the people she associates with," Fred defended.

"You don't understand the nature of these young ladies. Don't give your heart away, as they can be poisonous," his other friend warned.

"For Sarah, trust me, she's a wonderful girl. She's just eager to work in the mine and would go to great lengths to achieve that. If she's missing, she might be with a co-worker or somewhere quiet," Fred explained.

"Then I suggest you visit radio and television stations to announce her disappearance," his friend advised.

They agreed to visit a radio station and provide all the necessary details about Sarah's disappearance. The announcement would continue until she was found. Afterward, they shared light-hearted jokes and anecdotes, making light of the situation.

After work, Fred met with his friends under a tree and decided to visit a radio station. They huddled in one of their friends' cars and headed to the station to report Sarah's disappearance. They provided her full name, photos, the last place they saw her, and the outfit she was wearing at the time.

They recounted the details accurately to the radio station's secretary and paid a small fee to ensure the announcement would continue until Sarah was found. It was a reasonable arrangement, given that it would provide a cost-effective means of raising awareness about her disappearance.

On their way back home, they exchanged jokes, giving amusing names to people who might be interested in her romantically. This offered a lighter moment amid the seriousness of their situation. To describe her physical appearance, Sarah was a quintessential Ghanaian beauty.

Her features included a round face, pristine white teeth, shapely backside, smooth skin, and lovely legs. Her gait had an alluring sway that would capture anyone's attention. She possessed long, natural hair that she could style in various ways. Seeing her dressed in jeans for work was truly tempting, and it was impossible not to steal a second glance.

However, Sarah was now fighting for her life on a hospital bed, her condition grave. Fred and his friends had already departed for their respective homes, exhausted after a long and eventful day.

"Hello, good morning. How are you doing?" a caller's voice broke the moment.

"Good morning. I'm doing great by the grace of God. How about you?" Fred responded; his voice tinged with sleepiness.

"I'm also doing well, by the grace of God. I apologize for interrupting your sleep. I'm the receptionist at the radio station. You reported a missing young lady named Sarah. I have some good news for you," she explained.

"Good news? That's remarkably swift. You folks have done an incredible job. Please, share the good news. I'm all ears," Fred's drowsiness vanished, replaced by enthusiasm.

"Someone brought us footage of Sarah being hit by a car. She was nearly killed in front of the Sea Hotel. The car that hit her fled the scene without stopping. Fortunately, we have the car's license plate number and have reported it to the police for further investigations," she clarified.

"Alright… so where is Sarah?" Fred inquired anxiously.

"A taxi driver took her away, and at the moment, we don't know her whereabouts. We've started reaching out to hospitals to see if they have any information. That's the update we have for you," the receptionist informed him.

"Thank you very much for your outstanding work. I'll inform my friends about the latest developments. Please keep me informed if you come across any more information. I appreciate your efforts," Fred expressed his gratitude.

"You're always welcome. You can rely on us anytime," she assured before ending the call.

"How can this be good news when they haven't found her yet? What was Sarah doing at the hotel?

Was she meeting someone there? Or was she simply going there to relax and make new friends? I hope they catch the reckless driver who hit her and bring him to justice," Fred was full of questions that he needed answers to. He prepared to take a shower while still lost in his thoughts.

Issabella was already awake and ready to head to work. She had been praying for her national service to end so she could receive her appointment letter. After quickly drinking the cocoa beverage her mother had prepared, she announced her departure.

"Take care and stay away from bad influences, as they can corrupt good morals," her mother advised.

"Sure, Mom. Let Dad know I've left," she replied, rushing to catch the bus.

Issabella had already completed her assigned tasks for the day under the supervision of her manager. She had doubled her usual speed in completing her work, eager to seize the opportunity she had been given. Despite her friends' envy, none of them were putting in the effort because they knew they wouldn't be retained by the company after their national service.

A young man entered the office after knocking on the door.

"Excuse me, are you Miss Issabella Ansah?" he directed his question at Issabella.

"Yes, that's me. How can I assist you?" she responded, taken aback.

"I was sent by my boss from the human resource management department. He provided a description of you, so I was able to identify you. Please don't be alarmed. He asked me to inform you to bring your certificates and national identification card to work tomorrow. We'll process them for your induction next week. Don't forget to provide your bank account details as well," he conveyed the message.

"I already have all those documents. I've been carrying them with me to work since last week because I was told they'd be needed for the induction. Can we start the process now?" she eagerly inquired.

"I don't believe we can start the process right now. My dear, he would have instructed me to bring you along if he knew you had the documents with you. Please come to the office early tomorrow morning," he recommended.

"I'll be there. Thank you very much, and please convey my regards to your boss," she responded with a friendly smile.

Her friends were less pleased with how things were progressing for Issabella especially the male friends who had decided to resign from the job. Issabella excused herself and went to the restroom.

"That's a brilliant idea. It will ensure we secure jobs before our national service ends. What's the point of staying longer when we know we have no future here?" one of the guys vented, slamming the table.

Upon her return from the restroom, Issabella intended to address her friends, but their expressions were far from welcoming. Musa, who had slammed the table, looked particularly hostile. With a sigh, she decided against it and cleared her throat.

"I trust that my intentions are pure. I know this wound will eventually heal. The end of national service is approaching, and soon I'll be able to relax and breathe freely. I hope that God softens their hearts and blesses them with job opportunities. I'm not holding any grudges," Issabella spoke to herself and then headed to her supervisor's office.

"Charles, I asked you a question. The food you asked me to buy, is it for you or for Sarah?" Raymond asked, repeating his question.

"Boss, the food? It's for Sarah. She's not well, and a hearty meal will help her take her medication. The hot pepper will aid her recovery and give her strength," Charles explained.

"Who told you that Sarah needs fufu in her condition? Didn't I overhear a colleague advising you not to give her water, let alone food? I heard her as I was heading to the male ward to check vitals," the nurse interjected, sounding disappointed.

"No! she told me to bring her light soup this morning. I only thought it best to add the fufu. Afterall, what is light soup without fufu and a little hot pepper?" Charles argued.

"The IV fluids she's receiving are more nourishing than the fufu you're bringing. Our approach is based on comprehensive healthcare for our patients. Please don't let intuitions guide your decisions. Each patient's situation is unique," the nurse clarified.

Raymond and Charles exchanged glances, unable to find the right words. Charles seemed to question his own judgment, and Raymond remained at a loss for words.

"Boss, since the explanation is clear, can I have the food? I'm hungry. I haven't eaten since last night. Taking care of Sarah hasn't been easy," Charles said with a hopeful grin.

"Fortunately, I don't eat fufu. Otherwise, I would have eaten it just to teach you a lesson," the nurse chimed in, prompting a chuckle from Raymond.

"You're lucky I'm not fond of fufu. Otherwise, I would have beaten you to it. Anyway, enjoy your meal," Raymond said as he handed the food to Charles.

"Boss, any money for Sarah's expenses? I don't have any money on me, and with the escalating cost of drugs, I'm not sure we'll be able to make it through the next five years," Charles joked.

"I understand that the economy is challenging, but I don't delve into politics. We can only discuss matters of faith, not greedy politicians. I'll send some money to your account. Make sure to keep receipts for everything you purchase," Raymond cautioned.

"Receipts? Don't worry about that. I graduated with a degree in accounting from a renowned university. I'll make sure every receipt is stamped and properly documented," Charles assured.

"A degree in accounting? Impressive."

"Not just a degree, but with a specialization in Science and Information Technology. I also have an educational background and can even tutor your kids. Unfortunately, I don't have a certificate for that. Education is an innate talent for hustling."

"But how do you put that into practice? Teaching requires skills and knowledge," Raymond asked, surprised.

"Teaching is easier now, boss. I can teach anything. Even subjects like building and construction or home economics. You just need to study what you're planning to teach, walk into the classroom, and deliver. If a student asks a question you don't know, you can simply tell them to look it up online or consult a source like ChatGPT."

"Students googling questions in the middle of a class?" Raymond asked incredulously.

"Yes, boss. After all, what's the internet for if not for learning? In more challenging situations, you can assign the question as homework to the entire class. Our teachers have been doing that, so why can't we adopt the same approach?" Charles explained with confidence.

"Your perspectives are quite diverse and unconventional. Every moment with you is a mystery. You're willing to do whatever it takes to survive. Your life is a collection of experiences but be cautious that they don't come back to haunt you in the future, my friend. Relying solely on past experiences can be risky. Don't open wounds you can't heal," Raymond advised.

"I'll bring you a book by Solomon Ezonle Akossey titled 'My Tears,' and I think you'll find it interesting. It might change some of your perspectives," Raymond suggested as he prepared to leave.

"Boss, don't forget about the money. I'll be waiting, and I promise to keep all the receipts safe for your review," Charles called out as Raymond started the car.

Thoughts of Rita still lingered in Raymond's mind. He was unsure whether to proceed with his plans or wait a bit longer. The memory of their kiss continued to haunt him, and he was torn about what to do. As he drove home, he checked his watch repeatedly, realizing that he was running late for work. He glanced at his phone and noticed a message from Mr. Ameyaw, but due to his tardiness, he ignored it and hurriedly headed home to freshen up.

Raymond finished dressing in his casual African long-sleeved shirt, and black neatly ironed trousers after about two minutes and quickly drove to the office in a speed of light. In about five minutes, he was already at the office compound.

"Look, my boss is here. I told you he'd arrive soon. Let me guide him to where he can park his car and then join you," Mr. Ameyaw announced, rushing over to Raymond.

"Good morning, sir, and welcome," Mr. Ameyaw greeted, retrieving his bag from the backseat.

"Good morning. How are you?" Raymond responded with a faint smile.

"Sir, oh, how can I not be well when you're dressed so nicely and smelling so good? I sent you…"

"A message, but I haven't had a chance to read it yet. I'll get to it once I'm settled in my office," Raymond interjected and attempted walking away.

"Sir, oh, don't worry about the message. The contents are right here," Mr. Ameyaw indicated, pointing to someone nearby.

"Who? The Abochi is the message content? What does that have to do with me this early morning?" Raymond questioned while looking at the direction.

"Oh! The message isn't for you; it's for me. I bought this phone from Abochi, and I said you'll pay him when you get here" Mr. Ameyaw happily said while showing the phone to Raymond.

"He explained that it's a fantastic phone with WhatsApp, which allows you to send messages, make calls, and even see the person you're talking to" Mr. Ameyaw elaborated with a sense of smile.

"He also mentioned something called Facebook and YouTube for social media and videos," Mr. Ameyaw added while busily examining the phone.

"Why didn't you call or text me before making such a purchase?" Raymond asked a bit furious.

"Was that ever my question, boss? I called you five times yesterday, and you didn't answer" Mr. Ameyaw retorted with a defensive face.

"I sent multiple messages, and you didn't reply. Abochi said this phone is in high demand, and this is the last one available in Ghana. If I don't buy it now, I'd miss out on using WhatsApp and other social media handles. Please pay him; he's been waiting for hours," Mr. Ameyaw explained.

"Abochi, how much is your phone?" Raymond inquired as he reached for his wallet.

9

The most elusive decisions often involve choosing between two options that are both good and right. It is not always a matter of distinguishing between good and bad or right and wrong.

The sweetest lips are those of a businessman advertising his products. They indeed belong to the most talented athletes, willing to go the extra mile for you to part with all the money you have.

"Please, it's three million walayi," Abochi said while kissing his finger and raising it up.

"Three million cedis? Is that an iPhone? Let me have a look," Raymond asked with curiosity.

He took the phone, and the box was labeled "iPhone," but the device itself had "fone" inscribed on it.

"Two different companies, Fone and iPhone originally made it. He even said it has a Wi-Fi connection with which I wouldn't have to buy data for the rest of my life. He supplies phones to big people in Ghana. Please pay him so I can start using my phone," Mr. Ameyaw interrupted.

"A phone made by two companies, and you believed him? Raymond questioned staring straight into Mr. Ameyaw's eyes.

"Abochi, do you mean the phone costs three hundred cedis?" Raymond turned his attention to Abochi and asked.

"Yes! You will give me three of these," Abochi replied, showing one hundred cedis note.

"He adds zero to any amount he says. He is talking about three hundred cedis. Please pay him so he can leave," Mr. Ameyaw said and happily placed the phone in a white polythene bag.

Raymond paid the money and after, he couldn't contain his laughter. Mr. Ameyaw thanked Abochi and asked him to bring some accessories for the phone when he finds them at the market. He also thanked Raymond for paying for his new phone.

"Don't mention it, Mr. Ameyaw. I'm sure your phone will even have an iron and refrigerator because these companies are very powerful" Raymond said with a touch of exaggeration and playfulness.

"A phone made by two wonderful companies. This is the first time I'm hearing such," Raymond chuckled.

"Sir, oh, every new thing becomes a mystery. Very soon, Richie, the janitor, will come asking me where

I bought mine" Mr. Ameyaw expressed, still being delusional.

"I know most people will also come begging to use some of my Wi-Fi because I won't buy credit for the rest of my life," Mr. Ameyaw continued with conviction.

"I hope you took Abochi's number, and do you have money for repairs?" Raymond continued laughing.

"Sir oh, Rita came here yesterday evening and this morning too" Mr. Ameyaw quickly chipped to change the subject.

"She was looking for you and stayed for a while before leaving to run an errand for someone. She requested that you call her as soon as you arrive," he continued.

"An errand? Did she mention where she was going to?"

"Yes, an errand and eerrrm…" Mr. Ameyaw stammered.

"Who is it? A male or female?" Raymond asked.

"She didn't say anything to me, oh. I tried to persuade her, but she didn't say anything. I swear, boss. You know she has been secretive since she started working here," Mr. Ameyaw explained.

"Ah! But you just told me she told you something, and now she didn't tell you anything? It was a guy, right?" Raymond inquired.

"Boss, let me check your pulse to see if you truly care about Rita or not" Mr. Ameyaw pretended to check his boss' pulse by holding his wrist.

"She's just a beautiful lady. I'm old. I might have taken the chance. If she agreed, I wouldn't mind having her as my second wife," Mr. Ameyaw joked.

"Do you have the financial means to support a lady like Rita? Can you afford her lifestyle, including her hair and even her cosmetics?" Raymond spoke out of emotions without facts.

"21st century ladies are expensive. Even their accessories are costly because they say they shine like diamonds. Mr., I would advise you to stay away from her and every lady you see around. They might look decent and humble, but they often have complex demands. Anything related to money, they are ready to take without considering the consequences," Raymond alleged, reminiscing the experience he had of Rita and the strange guy.

"You are right, my boss, but for every lady on earth, God has created a special man to look after her. There are many women who would appreciate me" Mr. Ameyaw said confidently.

"I know money matters, but there's something greater that can win them over. I don't take chances when I have a lady in my life. Before she exits, she'll ask when I'll invite her again. I don't compromise on my love life, even at my age," Mr. Ameyaw declared, trying to relive his glory days with a hint of exaggeration.

"Are you trying to say you've been cheating on your wife?" Raymond angrily inquired.

"No, we've both been cheating on each other. She thinks I don't know. She's been sneaking into the room of our next-door neighbor. I caught her three times and pretended not to notice. I asked her, and she scolded me for not buying a television for the house" he explained.

"So, she goes there to watch television?" Raymond asked for clarification.

"That's what she claimed, but it's clear that they were using that as an excuse to spend time together. That's what led me to start cheating, and I'm grateful for that decision. Once a lady starts cheating, you better watch out, boss. She can sleep with a man right under your nose," Mr. Ameyaw narrated.

Mr. Ameyaw was sharing his wisdom about modern women with Raymond. He pointed out various signs of troubled relationships that shouldn't be taken to the level of marriage. Raymond wanted to ask about what he had witnessed between Rita and Paul, but he hesitated.

"Mr. Ameyaw, I was thinking that the day..." Raymond began, only to be interrupted.

"Let me share a strange sign that you should watch out for when considering marrying a woman," Mr.

Ameyaw said, grabbing Raymond's attention just as he was about to end the conversation.

"Women will always be women, and nothing can change that. They can lie to you without even realizing it, especially when emotions are involved. They can go to great lengths to make you believe everything they say. If you see her with another man at night, she's likely cheating," Mr. Ameyaw stated.

"What if it's her brother or a family member?" Raymond asked, taken aback.

"Even then! She might be cheating, so you should be cautious or avoid her altogether. Love is most genuine when it's guided by your heart rather than your mind. I almost lost my mind when my girlfriend broke up with me. Be careful with whom you give your heart to, boss," Mr. Ameyaw elaborated.

At the hospital, Charles was sitting by Sarah's left-hand side. She looked better than the day before, but the doctor had recommended she stayed under observation for some time. Charles was delighted because this meant he could spend more time away from work while getting paid by Raymond to take care of Sarah.

"Fuel prices have gone up again, and passengers have resorted to walking rather than taking cars. They're even asking for free rides, especially the elderly and the attractive ladies," Charles muttered to himself.

"Let me call the medicine counter assistant and get some prescriptions. She's a lovely girl, and I must get closer to her, no matter what. She seemed interested in my car keys, so she must have interest in me. Women and cars," he chuckled and took out his phone to call her.

Charles excused himself from Sarah and dialed her number.

"Hello, this is Charles. I was at your pharmacy yesterday evening. Do you remember me?" he asked, smiling sheepishly.

"Many people came to the pharmacy last night, and I can't recall everyone's voice. What did you purchase?" she inquired.

"I was the guy with the car keys" Charles quickly interjected.

"Oh, I remember now. Charles, right? I was expecting your call. You said you had something to discuss. How have you been?" she asked.

"I'm doing well, my dear. Anyway, I didn't catch your name," Charles replied.

"My name is Agnes..." she started introducing herself, but paused because she had to attend to a customer who had just walked in.

"Sorry, can you hold on for a moment? I have a customer here," she said.

"No problem, take your time," Charles responded, waiting patiently.

"Charles, I apologize for keeping you waiting on the call. You know that in every business, customer satisfaction is the primary goal, right?" Agnes asked rhetorically trying to make up for the lost time.

"Yes, dear. I would wait an eternity for you if it meant you'd be with me," Charles said, feeling hopeful.

"Please don't flatter me with your sweet words. Men in cars often try to take advantage of women. But thank you for being patient on the call for more than twenty minutes. How can I assist you?" Agnes asked as she continued organizing drugs on the shelves.

"Nothing now! Since I got your number, I haven't called to add it to my contacts. So, I decided to respect humanity and save it. Also, I don't use my car to win affection. My car is a part of my life because I work with it, not to manipulate women into sleeping with me," Charles explained while peering through the hospital door.

"Agnes, the way you sound suggests that you're speaking from experience. Have you been a victim of a man who used his car to manipulate you into bed?" Charles asked with certainty.

Fred called his friends and shared the news with them. They were extremely excited about the update, expressing their eagerness to find her sooner than expected.

"I don't think she can stay with me when she returns from wherever she went. I don't know any of her relatives, and if something like this happens again, I might have a big problem to deal with," Fred disclosed to his friends.

"You mean to say she has been staying with you without you knowing any of her relatives?" a friend asked.

"You only truly understand pain when it affects you directly. Because you enjoy an innocent lady's company for free, you choose not to find out more about her? Men and their shallow behavior," another friend teased.

"Are you both talking out of experience? Fred questioned.

"Just because no lady escapes your lustful desires, you think every man is like you, right? She never allowed me to cross any boundaries, not even a simple kiss, let alone anything more intimate. She is a very decent lady," Fred clarified.

"If you're so sure, then hold your scrotum and squeeze it hard," his friend challenged while laughing sarcastically.

"Friends let's not make this personal. I don't intend to engage in any debates. You can choose to believe me or not. I just received a notification from my network provider that my airtime is about to run out. Let's continue this conversation tomorrow at work, and if there's any significant news from the radio station, I'll share it on WhatsApp," Fred affirmed, having a mix of emotions. They all agreed and ended the call.

Issabella had already arrived home and checked her files to ensure her certificates were in order. She arranged them neatly and checked each one carefully. She cleaned her shoes and ironed her dress, knowing that there might be an interview after the medical examination. She then headed to the kitchen to prepare a meal for the family.

The table was set after thirty minutes, and they all gathered to eat. Issabella's mother said a short prayer.

"Lord, bless the farmer, the cook, and the one who eats," she prayed, and the family responded with "Amen."

After ten minutes of eating, Issabella's father broke the silence.

"I don't think this decision of yours is wise. You need to reconsider" he said placing the spoon on the empty plate.

"Are you talking about her working at the mining company?" her mother asked, surprised, and swallowed the remaining food in her mouth.

"No, it's high time you sat down with your daughter as a woman and educated her on bringing a man into the house. She's now grown enough to earn her own income and not rely on me. Why then is she not in a relationship?" Issabella's father inquired.

"Are you suggesting she should get married at the age of twenty-five? Issabella's mother asked, feeling enraged and paused eating.

"She started school early, so don't assume that makes her ready for marriage," she added, sounding frustrated.

"Yes! She should be settled in her husband's home by now. Sherry got married at twenty-four, and you were present at her wedding. Angie also got married at twenty-two after getting pregnant by that wealthy man" her dad argued in an angry tone.

"Dad, are you indirectly saying I should get pregnant by a wealthy man?" Issabella asked incredulously.

"No, I didn't mean a wealthy man, just a rich man. Don't think I'm talking about that Muslim friend of yours who married at twenty. Even though she didn't finish school, she's married now and living with her husband. I don't think it's a bad idea anyway," her father clarified.

"I don't think the man I married is sitting at this table with me right now. Are you that heartless? If I knew this was the future, I wouldn't have allowed you touch me to conceive this wonderful girl, only for her to be treated like this in the name of marriage," her mother protested indignantly.

"This is a clear shadow of the past" she sobbed, whipping her face with a tissue.

"Woman! I married you, not the other way around. You better respect my opinions or keep quiet and let me manage my family the way I see fit. If you're tired of this marriage, please..." he stopped abruptly.

Issabella was waiting anxiously for answers, but her mother couldn't hold back her tears. She hadn't wanted to reveal all of this, but the "I am the man of the house" attitude had pushed her to her limit, especially when her husband refused to listen to anyone else's opinions.

"Everything I did was for the well-being of our family, until they admitted your mother to the hospital. She has been the woman I've loved since we met. I gave her everything, and she did the same for me. My love for her was beyond comprehension, but I couldn't handle the emotional turmoil when her family ignored their responsibilities, fully aware of my financial situation," he explained, his voice breaking.

"I did what I did because I missed the physical intimacy we once shared. My niece had a similar figure, and her appearance was attractive whenever she emerged from the bathroom..." he was interrupted.

"So, Dad, you had a sexual relationship with her in your marital home?" Issabella asked, her shock evident.

"No, my daughter, we didn't do that in our marital bed. It's regrettable to admit that we engaged in such behavior on the floor. I know it was wrong, but have you ever asked your mother what happened between her and Pastor Ezekiel? They were involved in a relationship right under my nose, but I chose to ignore it," Issabella's father admitted with a hint of shame.

"I pretended that everything was fine and waited patiently to see how it would unfold. If you have clothes that are dirty and torn, you wouldn't hang them outside, right? Similarly, I questioned whether you are truly my daughter," he added, his tone serious.

"Me? Not your daughter, Dad? All my friends often mention how much I resemble you, and Mum too. Mum, please, can you tell me who my father is?" Issabella asked, tears streaming down her face.

"We may have resemblances because we've spent so many years together. I received a call from your grandmother when I was on a journey to Accra. She informed me that your mother was pregnant, and the ultrasound confirmed it was a girl. I was surprised that the call came from your grandmother and not your mother. Nevertheless, I accepted the news and continued my journey, unable to discuss it further on public transportation," Issabella's father explained.

"I stayed in a hotel upon arriving. That night, lying in bed, I thought about my pregnant wife. Six years of marriage without a child had been difficult, and I knew that this child was not biologically mine," he continued.

"But Dad, sometimes God works in mysterious ways, and I believe this was a miracle."

"It's a miracle, my daughter! If God had sent you and answered prayers with a blaze of glory, He would have given me a son, not a daughter. Every time I prayed, I asked Him to bless me with a fine and handsome son," he concluded.

"Mum, please, can you tell me who my real father is?" Issabella pleaded, deeply shaken by the revelations.

"Dad!! Please tell me that all these are just accusations born from anger. I believe that you always act in our best interest. Please tell me that dad is not telling the truth," Issabella asked, her concern evident.

10

We often find ourselves getting upset over trivial matters that we should simply dismiss and move on from. We waste countless hours dwelling on grudges and grievances that will ultimately be forgotten by us and others in a year's time. Instead, we should devote our time and energy to worthwhile pursuits such as noble actions, positive emotions, profound thoughts, and long-term commitments.

Agnes remained silent on the phone for a moment, pondering over what to say to Charles. She had long wanted to confide in someone she could trust, and finally, she found an opportunity to express the painful experience of being used and discarded by a man she had deeply fallen in love with.

"Charles, there's something I need to share with you. I met a very handsome man who caught my attention when I was working as a cleaner in a supermarket. He was wealthy, drove fancy cars, and fulfilled my childhood dream of sitting in the front seat of a luxurious car. He showered me with love and attention that any woman would desire," Agnes explained.

"I had little to offer as he was already financially well off. I found myself mostly receiving in the relationship. One day, in an attempt to prove my love and commitment, I offered him my virginity. The pain I experienced was so intense that I couldn't even walk home that night. I ended up staying with him for five days. We were intimate for an extended period, and his constant praise made me addicted to him," she continued in a soft voice.

"So, you became his pastime?" Charles interjected, positioning the phone well on his left ear.

"Long story short, the situation turned worse when he started bringing other women to his place. He took advantage of them as well. He persuaded me to quit my job, promising to take care of me. I lost the house my boss had provided for me, and he manipulated me emotionally," Agnes narrated.

"Agnes, I don't dwell on the past. I believe the past guides our path and makes us stronger for the future. Now, I need a favor from you," Charles said.

"A favor? Tell me more. If I can help, I will," Agnes offered.

"I need you to create some receipts and drug prescriptions for me. Total them to two thousand cedis."

"Two thousand cedis? Are you planning to rob a company? And what's in it for me?" she asked candidly.

"I'm not robbing anyone dear. I'm an unemployed graduate trying to improve my life. Someday, I'll explain more. Add an extra five hundred cedis to that amount, that's your share," Charles explained.

He requested that Agnes quickly generate the receipts as he was on his way. Her initial disbelief turned into a willingness to help due to the prospect of obtaining two months' worth of salary from a single deal.

"Making money that equals two months' salary in one deal is worth the risk. After all, what do I stand to lose? Let me get this done quickly," Agnes thought to herself as she prepared the receipts.

"My boss, keep your eyes open before someone takes away the car you bought with your hard-earned money," Mr. Ameyaw advised and left for his security post.

Raymond arrived at his office, grappling with his feelings about Rita. He had lost interest in their relationship and had decided to concentrate on taking care of Sarah. Rita had already received money from Paul and was planning her business expenditures. She checked her phone, noticing no messages or missed calls from Raymond.

"I don't believe marriage guarantees a place in heaven. What good is it for a man to marry the devil and lose his place in heaven? Heaven is my eternal home, and I need to carefully consider my decisions," Raymond contemplated.

Raymond found himself in a state of confusion regarding Rita's behavior. His thoughts drifted from Rita to Sarah and then to Irene, a former girlfriend who had broken his heart.

Raymond's reminiscences took him back to his school days. He recalled his relationship with Irene, a demanding woman who seemed to compete with everyone around her. Despite her beauty and intelligence, their relationship faltered because of her insistent material demands.

Amid these memories, Raymond pondered the situation with Rita. He couldn't help but feel drawn to Sarah as a potential partner. He also considered the cold treatment he had received from Sarah and his disillusionment with her.

"As for Rita, she kissed another man right in front of me. She's been avoiding my calls and even lied to me about being with a man on our date," he murmured to himself.

"Issabella, you must believe what I'm about to tell you. As your mother, I want you to listen carefully..." her mother began, her voice full of emotion.

"Pastor Ezekiel was making advances towards me consistently. He was the main reason I changed my phone number. Yes...! We had some interactions, but they occurred when your father began displaying unwarranted behavior towards me," she paused.

"I never engaged in any physical intimacy with Pastor Ezekiel. We only kissed, and I'm certain that the devil was at work. He confided in me about the division within the church. He was burdened by pressure from church leaders. That evening, I was watching my usual TV show in his room. Suddenly, the lights went out, and the next thing I remember is where I had thrown my clothes," she revealed feeling uneasy on her seat.

"But Mum, you went to a man's room to watch TV? Wasn't there a television at home? I'm confused," Issabella asked, clearly surprised with her eyes widely opened.

"You're fortunate to see this house transformed so remarkably. Your father sold everything he could to provide for me during my illness. I'm grateful for his love, but I worry that he couldn't remain faithful for those few years," Issabella's mother explained in a shaky voice.

"Regarding your question, the man sitting here is your father" her mother strongly confirmed, slapping the dining table consecutively.

"We engaged in an affair two weeks before he traveled. I noticed the miscarriages were likely due to excessive happiness, so I decided to keep this news to myself" she continued looking in the direction of her husband.

"My daughter, that's the explanation I have. As for marriage, your father might be the head of this household and even the king of heaven, but you won't be getting married anytime soon until the right man comes along and…" Just before she could complete her statement, her husband jumped in.

"So, you're conspiring with your daughter to deny me my responsibilities?" He angrily said.

"Fine, you'll be the head of this household since I have no say here. You'll manage every aspect of this house. I don't even know if marrying you was a mistake or not," her father continued angrily, attempting to leave the dining table.

"I see where all these arguments are leading. I'll decline the job offer from the mining company. To bring happiness to this family, I think I must be the savior and sacrifice my future," Issabella declared sounding angry.

"Don't you dare make such a decision" her father shouted.

"You'll do as I say. Will you repay all the money I've spent on your education? You're taking on the work, providing for the family, and then planning to marry later" her mother insisted rising from the chair.

"You're not matured enough to build a family. Marriage isn't a game for the inexperienced," her mother snapped, leaving the table.

"But Dad, aren't you going to say anything...?"

"My daughter, for peace to prevail in this house, follow your mother's wishes. Otherwise, she'll raise hell. She speaks as if I haven't played a role in your life. That's life for you! Get ready and take on the path to success. I believe you'll make me proud someday," Issabella's father encouraged her, holding her tightly.

"I'll make you proud, Dad," she replied and left for her room.

The radio station's secretary had provided an address where Sarah could be found. Fred and his friends arrived at the hospital to visit her. They expressed their sympathy and gratitude for Charles' care and attention to Sarah's recovery. Charles recounted his efforts and expenses, sharing a long list of costs along with a receipt.

"We're grateful for taking care of our sister. You've spent considerable time with her here. We came as soon as we got the address from the radio station to confirm her admission. We've brought this envelope, and we'll be fully prepared by Sunday," Fred said, signaling their intention to provide financial support.

After thanking them and reminding them about their visit on Sunday, Charles bid them farewell.

Sarah tried to wave at them but was interrupted by a severe coughing fit. She indicated to Charles to reduce the fan's speed, which he promptly did.

Meanwhile, Rita had come to a decision regarding her romantic life. She vented her frustration about Raymond's behavior and firmly resolved to choose Paul as her partner.

"After weighing all the factors, I'll marry Paul" she said to herself, feeling a sense of relief for the decision she had made.

"I've known him for years, even before our breakup. I owe him this chance to see if things can work out in marriage. My friends are getting married left and right and Raymond isn't giving me the attention and affection I crave. He's always busy with work or attending lengthy church activities. Marriage should be enjoyed, not endured," Rita exclaimed, pacing her room.

"I won't think about this any longer. I need to inform the pastor of my decision, and then I'll let Raymond know. I don't even like the attitude of the church members anymore" she positively asserted to herself throwing her hands in the air.

"I'm seriously considering leaving for an English-speaking church nearby. I want a church that discusses various aspects of life and makes you feel like family" she added and turned on the television.

"They ask questions and expect answers, as if they have control over you. I can't continue worshipping in such a place," she ranted, still pacing.

She decided to call the pastor and explain her decision. The pastor, however, encouraged her to attend the upcoming night vigil and emphasized the importance of spiritual matters over material gains.

Charles and Raymond were engaged in a phone conversation, with Charles providing updates about Sarah's health. Raymond was elated to hear that Sarah had mentioned his name and shared a few details about her condition. He confirmed that he would visit as soon as his office work was completed.

"Why is Rita calling me?" Raymond questioned as he took the phone away from his ear following continuous beeps during his call.

"Rita? Who's that? Your girlfriend?" Charles inquired upon hearing the name.

"Sorry, it's nobody. Let's get back to our conversation. Please let Sarah know I'll be there in the evening. Has she taken all her medications this afternoon?" Raymond asked with some sense of joy.

"I have a dislike for women named Rita. They tend to be dishonest and lack candor. The Ewes who choose such names for their children have different intentions compared to other tribes" Charles explained while looking at a nurse who walked by.

"Boss, let me tell you, a certain Rita once broke my heart so badly that it drove me crazy. I wouldn't want you to experience the same pain I went through," Charles revealed.

"But why are we even discussing Rita? I assigned you one simple task – to inform Sarah. Are you now eavesdropping on my conversation? Is that what you were taught?" Raymond's irritation was evident.

"No, I apologize, boss. Please forgive me. I'll pass on the message to Sarah as soon as she wakes up. Also, I purchased some medication for Sarah yesterday. I'll send you the receipts so you can reimburse me. I need to send money to my parents for their medication and household expenses," Charles added pulling his tongue.

"Scan the receipts to my email. I'll send you the money right away. Take care of yourself and especially Sarah. May God bless you abundantly for your dedication."

"Boss, when you send the money, please include the charges as well. Also, about our earlier conversation, can we continue that when you visit?" The call ended before Raymond could hear the last statement.

A few hours before the end of the workday, Mr. Ameyaw struggled with his phone charger and socket. He went outside his security post to check another socket, but the issue persisted. He summoned Malik, the new gardener hired after the previous one, Musa, who passed away a week ago.

"Malik, could you please help me charge my phone at your end?" Mr. Ameyaw politely requested.

"Of course, hand it over, and I'll charge it for you," Malik agreed.

"Thank you very much. Please be careful with the phone; it's quite expensive. My plugs seem to have trouble charging because the phone is very quality. You can ask boss Raymond; he's the one who bought it for me."

"Take your time as you insert the charger into the socket. Gently place the phone down and let it charge," Mr. Ameyaw cautioned.

"Your phone isn't charging; it keeps connecting and disconnecting," Malik informed.

"Can you read the pop-up messages?"

"I'm sorry, but I completed school at an unusually young age before becoming a hustler. I think there's an issue with my socket as well. Maybe you could try the reception or a different spot," Malik suggested.

"I'm not fond of the receptionist's attitude. She seems to think beauty involves applying red lipstick and excessive makeup" Mr. Ameyaw said clearly rejecting the option.

"Let me mind my own business. The problem isn't with my socket; is it that the socket can't handle the quality of my phone? I'll send it to Raymond; he might be able to help," Mr. Ameyaw concluded and left with his phone and charger.

Issabella had completed all her tasks at work, receiving an offer letter that detailed her job responsibilities and a range of allowances she could enjoy after her three-month probation. It was a promising moment for her. She formed new friendships, primarily with men as her workplace was male dominated.

During her breaks, Issabella often contemplated ways to bring happiness to her parents. Her mother was interested in financial support for the household, while her father was eager for her to find a husband. Although both were important to her, she believed these goals could be achieved one step at a time.

After a few minutes, a young and attractive guy approached her in the cafeteria. He introduced himself, initiated a conversation, exchanged contact information, and left. Issabella felt tensed during the encounter and couldn't speak much. Soon after, her phone rang and vibrated. The young man signaled that he was the caller, and the call ended. It was evident that this encounter was a novel experience for her.

Back in his office, Raymond heard a knock and granted entry to the person. It was Mr. Ameyaw, who had a request.

"Sir, I'm sorry to bother you, but could you please charge my phone for me?" Mr. Ameyaw asked.

"Why? What's wrong with the sockets in your office?" Raymond inquired, engrossed in his files.

"Sir, I don't know ooh, but my original phone isn't charging. I suspect the socket isn't authentic. You know management often provides us with substandard equipment. I trust that your socket can effectively charge my phone so I can make some calls before heading home," Mr. Ameyaw explained.

"Use the socket behind you, but please be cautious not to accidentally unplug my printer. And on your way out, could you bring me a cup of coffee?" Raymond instructed.

"Sir, I'm encountering the same pop-up message again. I apologize for disturbing you, but could you please take a look?" Mr. Ameyaw called Raymond's attention, seeming worried.

"It's displaying a red caution triangle. Is it undergoing an update? Abochi mentioned that the phone might automatically download information to iCloud," Mr. Ameyaw inquired as he plugged the charger into the socket.

Raymond burst into laughter, struggling to contain himself. He took the phone in his hand, his amusement evident.

Mr. Ameyaw was perplexed by the reaction. He attempted to read the pop-up message but couldn't comprehend it. Raymond's laughter persisted.

"Your phone is charging the charger and the socket. Hahahaa..." Raymond managed to articulate between bouts of laughter.

"Are you saying my original phone is charging the charger and your socket?" Mr. Ameyaw asked, astonished.

"Yes, that's exactly it!" Raymond confirmed, still chuckling.

"You must be saying this out of envy. So, which office has the best socket?"

"You can head to the Manager's office to charge your phone. You'll be grateful when you return downstairs. I warned you against buying this phone from Abochi. This phone can seemingly charge both the socket and the charger. Do you think that's a good phone?" Raymond's laughter continued.

"Raihaana, can you bring me a cup of hot coffee?" Raymond requested on the phone and ended the call.

"Thank God you're here, Raihaana. Could you please read the caution message on the phone for me?" Mr. Ameyaw asked the secretary and connected the charger to the phone.

Upon seeing the message, Raihaana's eyes lit up, and she instructed Mr. Ameyaw to disconnect and reconnect the charger. She held the phone and burst into laughter before swiftly leaving the office without inquiring about Raymond's coffee preference.

"Why did she leave laughing? Well, I know who's jealous. Raihaana can't stand that I'm using an authentic phone from two companies – iPhone and fone. My God will always bless me and elevate me from glory to glory," Mr. Ameyaw remarked in a hushed tone.

"Do you trust Abochi more than the person who bought you the authentic phone? I'm telling you the truth, and Raihaana's reaction affirms it," Raymond stated.

"Mr. Ameyaw, please tell me who sold you this phone. It's undeniably an inferior product. How can a phone charge both the charger and the socket? Hahahaaa... the sockets here are genuine. Alternatively, you can charge it at home when you're there," Raihaana advised, returning with Raymond's coffee. The two joined in the laughter.

On the phone...
Charles: Hello, Sunshine, how are you?

Agnes: I can't be anything but well when my angel is doing fine.

Charles: Hahahaha... you really know how to flatter me. I want to express my sincere gratitude for the receipts, and I'm excited about the potential for further collaboration between us. Soon, we could even establish a proper business venture together because you're an exceptional businesswoman. It's a shame your boss fails to recognize your immense potential. If I were in his position, I'd have made you the manager, not just an ordinary salesgirl.

Agnes: My dear, I also enjoy working with you. If for nothing else, I'm eagerly anticipating receiving twice a full month's pay. Thank you for coming into my life.

Charles: You're most welcome, Sunshine. Your share will be with you soon. On that note, can you prepare three more receipts for this week?

Agnes: Consider it done. Swing by this evening to pick them up; my boss will be leaving early today.

Charles: Alright, I'll be there.

11

Every action we take is a result of our own desires and decisions, regardless of whether we claim otherwise. While we may rationalize our choices by saying we had no other option or that we were coerced, the truth is that we always have the power to choose for ourselves. Ultimately, the power to make choices lies solely within us.

Mr. Ameyaw had indeed backed the wrong horse. After Raihaana confirmed the pop-up message on his original phone, he was left unsure of what to do. He gracefully unplugged his phone from the socket and left without saying a word. He quietly returned to his post, examining the phone from various angles.

In less than five minutes, Mr. Ameyaw's name changed to "original." Annoyed and left with no choice, he had to accept and respond to his new name. He contemplated searching for Abochi to reclaim his money, but the number he had been given was unreachable.

Raymond had finished his tasks on his desk and promptly responded to an email he had received.

Another message arrived shortly, but he chose to ignore it and left the office to visit Sarah.

Issabella's father was plagued by a sudden sense of guilt for how he had treated his niece. He had harshly cast her out of his house, and since then, he hadn't taken any steps to search for her. Although she was his only family, he had shown little concern. As he thought about the places she might have gone, he realized that most of her childhood friends in the community had either moved away or gotten married.

"Where could Adepa be?" he murmured to himself. He stood in front of the opened window in his bathroom.

"The pain is too much to bear" he continued and clenched his fist in sorrow.

"I turned her away due to my selfish desires. My own niece! and I even attempted to do something inappropriate with her. How did she find shelter that night?" tears rolled down his cheeks uncontrollably and he wiped some off with the back of his right hand.

"I left her at the mercy of those troublemakers who had just been released from prison" he said this while hitting the wall with the clenched fist.

"She might still be out there, struggling to make ends meet. Here I am, in this big house, while my only family member is suffering. What came over me in that moment?" he added very morosed.

"My cruelty is haunting me now. I have a loving wife and a talented daughter, yet our home is not at peace. Where can I find Adepa?" Issabella's father mourned.

He considered discussing the matter with his wife but hesitated. He believed it would be wiser to talk to his daughter, Issabella, first. If she agreed to help find Adepa, he could avoid his wife's anger.

Issabella's Father: Issa, may I speak with you?

Issabella: Sure, Dad.

Issabella's Father: First, I want to apologize for the wrongs I've committed against you and your mother. My selfish desires led me astray, and I even treated my only niece unfairly. I'm tormented by my actions and don't deserve to be called a father.

I'm in a state of devastation due to my mistakes. I'm asking for your forgiveness and urging you to help me seek your mother's forgiveness as well. This wound won't heal unless all three of you forgive me. I promise not to pressure you into early marriage, and I'm willing to respect your mother's opinions and emotions in our decisions.

Issabella: but Dad, who's Adepa?

Issabella's Father: She's, my niece. My only sister died at a very young age, and I promised to take care of her only child who was 10 years old then. One night, I was drunk and attempted to take advantage of her. Upon several refusals, I threw her out of the house, and I haven't attempted to look for her till now and it's been 10 years! He was now weeping as a child.

Issabella's Mother: My dear, to err is human, but to forgive is divine. I understand your feelings deeply. I forgive you for all the pain you've caused. Let's work together to rebuild our happy family. I, too, seek your forgiveness, my husband.

She had been eaves dropping the entire time because she suspected her husband to coerce their daughter into getting married.

Issabella's Father: I forgive you, my love.

Issabella cleared her throat, feeling a bit uncomfortable with the emotional atmosphere. She felt a tinct of relief then.

Issabella: Can you both spare me the dramatics, please? Since we're all committed to making things right, I propose we search for Adepa together. I'm willing to help fund the inquiries, and I'm confident we can find reliable sources. We'll locate her soon.

Issabella's Father and Mother: God bless you, our daughter.

After showering Issabella with blessings, they all broke into tears once again.

"I never knew my parents were capable of such drama. Well, I'm glad they're reconciling. My greatest wish is to find my cousin," Issabella sighed heavily.

Three weeks later...

Issabella and her family had initiated the search for Adepa. Issabella played a key role in the search and tried all avenues possible to locate her cousin.

"Someone wants to speak with you," the speaker said, handing the phone to another person.

"Alright, but who am I speaking with?" Issabella inquired.

She had just returned from break and was waiting for a call from the police owing to an earlier assurance by the head of police to call in the morning.

"Hello, Issabella. You can hold off on the questions for now," the voice on the other end said.

There was silence on the line.

"I can imagine you're quite surprised to hear from me. Although we don't know each other, I can sense your kind nature."

"Could you please identify yourself?" Issabella inquired again.

"A watched pot never boils. You need to wait and hear me out" the caller said.

"I know you, but I haven't approached you due to our history. You might have noticed that I've always wished you well whenever you leave work. I've been observing you ever since you started working at the mines. I admit..."

"Wait, you've been stalking me?" Issabella interrupted.

"I understand that eavesdropping on your conversation was wrong. However, you'll appreciate my curiosity later. I didn't want to leave any trace, which is why I asked a colleague to call you from her phone. It's true that a good reputation is more valuable than riches. Your family has earned my forgiveness because of your remarkable behavior."

Issabella's voice softened as the speaker's tone became shaky.

"A wonderful and kind woman like you doesn't deserve to bear the consequences of the terrible actions of her father. I work the night shift as security guard at your workplace. This wound of mine needs to heal today. Please tell Uncle that I forgive him, and I wish you a happy home. These have been dark years since..."

The voice paused, overcome with emotion.

Issabella was utterly stunned.

"My dear, I'm profoundly sorry for the pain I've caused. However, there's one favour I'd like to ask of you" Issabella began, feeling completely sorrowful.

Could you allow me to pick you up this weekend and bring you to my house? My family would be honored to meet you. My father has been cruel to you, but this matter should be discussed within the family. I know you've just finished your shift today and will have the weekend off," Issabella implored.

Adepa agreed after contemplating her cousin's proposal.

During the late hours of Saturday, Issabella received a call from her cousin who informed her that she was at the junction she was asked to wait at. Issabella quickly informed her parents about her cousin's arrival and asked them to wait patiently.

"Dear, I'm truly honored and excited that you agreed to come home with me. You have a big heart. I want to take this moment to express my gratitude for your willingness to forgive. I had no idea you were this close to me," Issabella said few minutes after meeting Adepa. She gave her a warm hug and they walked towards the house.

"Life is meant to be embraced with an open heart, free from regrets. We have the power to decide how we live it" Adepa confessed and held Issabella by the hand.

"There are instances when we find ourselves entangled in suffering, betrayal, rejection, among other challenges. In such moments, it's important to exercise patience, forgiveness, and the resilience to overcome. These challenges can leave us with wounds that might never heal if we don't confront them," Adepa advised and smiled.

They arrived in less than 5 minutes.

"Please, have a seat and make yourself at home. My parents will be here soon," Issabella invited. She was very excited about the reunion and hoped all things will go well.

"Thank you." Adepa replied and sat down, lounging in the middle of the couch, leaning back against the cushions.

"So, how long have you been working in the mines?" Issabella asked, also sitting on the left side of the couch close to the armrest.

"It's been..." Adepa paused, trying to fight back her emotions.

Adepa's words trailed off as she noticed Issabella's parents entering the room. She was left speechless when she saw her uncle. Both parents seemed uncertain about how to approach and welcome her. Issabella's father, in particular, appeared profoundly shocked. He could hardly believe that his niece was in front of him after so many years. Adepa had blossomed into a beautiful woman with graceful curves. Her complexion radiated a healthy glow as if she had never been exposed to the sun. The room fell silent and tense. Everyone seemed frozen in place, unable to utter a word, as tears streamed down their cheeks.

"Should I fetch you some water?" Issabella broke the silence.

"I'm okay, thank you," Adepa replied while wiping away her tears.

A few weeks later, Rita appeared to have moved on from Raymond. Her relationship with Paul wasn't any better than before. Paul was known for frequently changing romantic partners, like how he changed his underwear. Although his lottery winnings kept him financially secured, his health had become a concern, leading him to leave home for reasons unknown.

Rita had attempted to contact Paul on all his phone numbers, but none of her attempts were successful. None of his female companions was also reachable. The fear of being deceived and manipulated once again haunted her. Her world was falling apart sooner than she had anticipated. Heretofore, her health hadn't been in good shape. She hadn't been physically active since she was still working on her business plan. She was mostly home and had grown to be very lazy. The Rita who used to work tirelessly throughout the day was now struggling even to get out of bed.

"Nurse Gina!!!" Sarah called out loudly to attract the attention of the nurse on duty. After weeks at the hospital, she had familiarized herself with the nurses on different shifts.

"Sarah, I think it's time for you to go home. You can't spend the rest of your life in this bed. What can I help you with now?" Nurse Gina asked.

"I need to use the restroom," Sarah replied in a pitiful tone while making an attempt to rise.

"Are you the alarm clock for the morgue? You've been waking up the dead. Have you spoken to Raymond yet?" the nurse inquired.

"No! I can't do that. I think Raymond is only being kind to me because I'm in a vulnerable state."

"As a friend, I'll advice you to talk to him. Raymond has a heart of gold. He's been taking care of you since the day you were brought here. He's been covering the cost of your medications and other expenses. Tell him the truth, and I'm sure he won't judge you. It's better to do it sooner rather than later," Gina advised.

"Let me assist you to the restroom. And wipe your tears before I kick you out," Gina teased.

Agnes had bitten off more than she could chew. Her dealings with Charles were spiralling into a nightmare. Her boss had detected the forgery and had started an investigation. He couldn't fathom why receipts had been issued for products that were never sold. Meanwhile, Charles was reaping the rewards of his actions and chasing after any money-making opportunities that came his way. He believed that Sarah's situation was his ticket to success, so he was determined to profit from it. A hungry wolf is never still.

"It's been a week now, and Charles hasn't shown up" Agnes muttered.

"Come to think of it, he's been ignoring my calls these days. Is this how he repays my kindness?" At this time, Agnes was starting to fume.

"I put my job on the line and forged receipts for him, and now he's turned the tables on me. My boss is investigating this thoroughly, while he's avoiding my calls" she said, her fume gradually turning into sadness.

"All my explanations and calculations are proving to be in vain. I haven't received a single penny from this embezzlement. Oh, God! Why did I get myself involved in this illegal act?" She asked rhetorically and put her right hand on her forehead.

"This Charles, or whatever his name is, better start praying that I don't get caught. Otherwise, he'll regret the day he set foot in this pharmacy," Agnes exclaimed from behind the counter.

"I apologize, ma'am; how may I assist you?" Agnes asked, shifting her focus.

"I've been standing here for a while, and you mean to tell me you didn't notice? Is this how you treat customers? Why bring your daydreaming to work? I'll report you to my husband because even a small fire can cause great damage. We can't afford to lose customers due to your lack of professionalism," Mrs. Offei complained amidst throwing her hands in the air.

"Ma'am, I..." Agnes attempted to speak but was shunned.

Mrs. Offei left the pharmacy without waiting for any explanations. Her anger clearly indicated her intention to complain to her husband.

The following day seemed a lucky day for Agnes. Customers seized not to rush in for drugs as if the country was plagued. She was enthused with the sales she had made in the early hours of the day. However, the thought of the ongoing investigation and its implications weighed her down.

"Agnes, I need you in my office immediately," Mr. Offei demanded, his anger evident.

"Of course, Sir," she responded anxiously.

"Good evening... I mean, sorry, good afternoon... No, good morning, Sir. How may I assist you?" Agnes stammered nervously.

"Agnes, spare the hypocrisy this morning" Mr. Offei slapped against his table.

"How could you be so cruel and deceitful? He yelled and stood abruptly.

"I am deeply disappointed in you, both as my employee and as the daughter of my best friend" Mr. Offei tried to control himself and moved a step backwards.

"I took you under my wings as a daughter to help you raise money for your education. Is this how you repay my kindness?" he asked rhetorically.

"I turned a blind eye to my wife's concerns about you because I had faith in your integrity. I believed you were a genuine, humble, reliable, and ambitious young woman striving to make ends meet. Yet, you've let me down so profoundly" he continued, feeling so disappointed.

"How could you issue receipts for such exorbitant amounts? Do you know something? I want you nowhere near my pharmacy again. You have twelve hours to pack your belongings and leave. Your actions warrant imprisonment for this illegal act" he slapped his desk again, throwing his hand in the air.

"If I return and find you here, I won't hesitate to have you locked behind bars," Mr. Offei yelled furiously and resumed his seat.

"Sir, please, I can explain..."

"Get out of my office now!!!" He slapped his hand on the desk repeatedly and then pointed his right hand to the door.

"Daavi, your son is here. I'll take the usual Monday dish, but make it extra spicy today," Charles relayed to the food vendor.

"Hahahahaha... Charles, you're too much. How can I add more spice to a dish that's already prepared?" Daavi retorted.

"Umm... my dear, give me a moment. When will my son, Raymond, come and settle his debt? It's been a while, and you know how tough times are now. Please tell him that I'm begging him to pay at least half of the money. Alternatively, you can give me his phone number, and I'll talk to him. My son isn't like this. Maybe he's facing financial difficulties."

"No... Daavi!!! Please leave that to me. I'll inform him, and as for his number, you don't need it. He'll pay you back before the sun sets." Charles quickly assured her.

Charles' deception had begun to catch up with him. Throughout Sarah's hospitalization, he had been using Raymond's name to buy food on credit. He took advantage of the familiarity between Daavi and Raymond to avoid paying immediately.

Raymond had visited Sarah and was concerned about her slow recovery.

"Hi, Sarah. How have you been?" Raymond greeted her, noticing her grim expression.

"I'm managing, thank you," Sarah replied weakly and forced a smile.

"I can see that you're not getting the care you need here. I'm thinking of transferring you to a better hospital where you can receive proper treatment and hopefully recover faster," Raymond suggested.

"Is he serious? Why does he want to transfer me now? Has someone told him that my condition is deteriorating?" Sarah wondered.

"What do you think about it?" Raymond asked, looking concerned.

Sarah was increasingly puzzled by his eagerness to move her to a different hospital.

"Umm... I think this hospital is fine. The doctors and nurses are competent, and they're providing proper care. I believe it's just a matter of time before I start feeling better," she reassured trying to sit up just to buttress her point.

"Has Charles brought your food today?" Raymond inquired.

"May I come in?" a familiar voice interrupted.

"Oh, look who's here at the mention of his name. Come in, Charles," Raymond welcomed and held him by the shoulder.

"I hope I'm not interrupting anything?" Charles questioned; his face adorned with a smile.

"You're right on time, Charles. I'm considering transferring Sarah to a different hospital to accelerate her recovery. What do you think?" Raymond asked.

"Boss, that's a considerate thought, but I don't think transferring her is necessary. This hospital is renowned for its exceptional healthcare, and the familiarity she has here will ensure her swift recovery. On another note, we should hear her preference" Charles explained.

"Anyway, the fuel efficiency of my car is limited for short distances, like from my house to the nearby food joint. Therefore, we might need to revisit my allowances as well," Charles added as he tried to find his balance by leaning close to a bed.

"Well, she prefers to be treated here," Raymond added.

"Alright. Maybe she should have something to eat now," Charles suggested.

Charles asked to be excused so he could pick up a call since his phone had been beeping throughout the time he was there.

On the phone...

"I'm currently not available, so could you send it to my apartment?" The voice on the phone stated.

"Wait, isn't that Frcd?" Sarah asked, surprised.

"Who!!! Fred????" Raymond questioned; anger evident in his voice.

12

Not every challenging path leads to ruin. Some may serve to challenge and cleanse the negativity within us, ultimately guiding us toward more fruitful endeavors once their lessons have been absorbed. Though wounds may heal quickly, they often leave behind lasting scars as reminders.

Rita had been having persistent diarrhoea which was not resolving with normal over-the-counter medications. She then sought medical attention and was diagnosed of HIV/AIDS. She couldn't accept this diagnosis and prayed fervently against it.

"How can I be HIV/AIDS positive? She questioned.

"I only contracted hepatitis B from Paul, but I've been receiving treatment for it. This must be a mistake! She tried to encourage herself.

"These young doctors nowadays can't be trusted. They're often chatting on their phones while diagnosing patients. How could she not make mistakes? I'll go for confirmation tomorrow," Rita protested.

Early the next morning, Rita hurriedly prepared and left for the hospital. She was amongst the first ten patients who waited for medical consultation. When it was finally her turn, she barged into the consulting room as if she was ready for a battle.

"Doctor, I came here complaining of a headache and fever, but the medications you prescribed are excessive. I also noticed that you had written 'HIV/AIDS positive' on my medical record, which I believe is a mistake due to your distracted state while writing. You were chatting on your phone during the process. I'm here to rectify this error," Rita unleashed a furious tirade, her words pouring out in an unbroken stream of anger.

"When was your last visit here?" the doctor inquired.

"Actually, just yesterday," she responded.

"Madam Rita, based on the laboratory test results, it appears that you have been infected with the HIV/AIDS virus. I recommend that you return home, follow the prescribed medications, and come back on the scheduled date. Alternatively, you can consider redoing the test at any laboratory," the doctor advised.

Tears welled up in Rita's eyes as she left the consultation room. She felt she had crossed a point of no return. Meanwhile, Paul had vanished without a trace. Two significant blows from the same person were too much for her to bear. With her hepatitis treatment yielding little success and now the prospect of starting HIV/AIDS treatment, she faced another challenging chapter.

"My beloved niece, my only family, Adepa... Your father is deeply sorry for his cruelty. I have hurt you greatly, and I don't deserve your forgiveness," Issabella's father sobbed.

Overwhelmed with emotion, he knelt before his niece, his tears flowing freely. Adepa was moved by his genuine remorse and how he sought to make amends. The family, sensing the opportunity to heal old wounds, also knelt before her, tears streaming down their faces. Adepa comforted them, assuring them that all was forgiven.

"Father, everything is fine," Adepa reassured him, also wiping away her tears.

The words "Father" from Adepa's lips melted away his tears. Her mother, too, expressed her remorse for her role in the past events.

"It's alright, please. Father, you can rise, and Mother, please take a seat," Adepa said.

Issabella and Adepa helped their parents up, and as they hugged each other, Adepa declared "no more tears." They settled down and engaged in a conversation. Adepa shared her experiences after the traumatic incident, how she had been silently watching over Issabella, and praised her cousin for her admirable behavior.

"By the way, cousin, you're young, beautiful, and intelligent. You're not rushing into marriage, are you?" Adepa inquired as she smiled and looked at her cousin.

The three of them exchanged glances, leaving Adepa suspicious of their demeanor.

"Or are you already married?" she probed.

"No, not at all. In fact,…" Issabella's voice trailed off.

Adepa sensed something was amiss from their reactions.

"Okay, that's good to hear. At your stage, society might expect you to bring a partner home, especially with your job at the mines and your age" Adepa said amid the tension.

"But my advice, as your sister, is to wait until you're genuinely ready. And to our parents, please don't pressure her into early marriage. She will find someone she loves and will introduce him to us when the time is right," Adepa advised.

"Thank you so much, my dear. We're grateful you've come home today, and we'll definitely heed your counsel," Issabella's father responded.

"Daughter, I've prepared an incredibly delicious local dish for the family. Would you stay and have a meal with us?" Issabella's mother invited.

"Of course, Mother," Adepa agreed.

Fred and Friends: Good day, everyone.
Charles and Sarah: Good day.
Upon the entry of Fred and his friends, Raymond's demeanor shifted. It had been a while since he last saw Fred after the incident at his house. The disdain on his face was apparent to everyone, and his clenched fist hinted at a brewing storm. Charles and his colleagues couldn't fathom Raymond's hostility and sudden change in mood.

"Ah, that reminds me. I guess you're here to fulfill the promise you made last time. I haven't forgotten about the money you owe me," Charles interjected, attempting to break the tension.

"This guy has been here before and no one informed me?" Raymond thundered.

"Boss, which one of them is..." Charles began.

"Keep quiet, Mr....!" Raymond's stern voice silenced him.

Raymond's anger was on the brink of eruption. He advanced towards Fred, gripping his shirt collar with an intensity that instilled fear in everyone. Charles hurriedly left to summon Nurse Gina since she had been fond of Sarah and expressed an unusual interest in her wellbeing. Fred's friends stood at a distance, wary of Raymond's fury. The situation was escalating rapidly.

"Tell me again why you're here after ruining Sarah's life!!! Speak before I break your bones!! Why are you even here!?" Raymond yelled at Fred.

Charles and Gina: Raymond!

"Raymond, stop!!" Sarah's voice rang out.

"Do you think this hypocrite deserves mercy, Sarah?" Raymond questioned, his anger unabated.

"He's not to blame," Sarah defended.

Raymond refused to relinquish his grip on Fred, disbelief in his eyes and ears. He turned and pounded the wall with his fist, channelling his anger into the solid surface. None could control him now. Gina dashed to find security personnel to defuse the situation.

"Are you going to save him from your own downfall, Sarah?" Raymond demanded, closing in on the bed.

"Please, hear me out, Ray," Sarah pleaded.

For the first time, Sarah addressed him as "Ray," signaling that something significant was about to unfold. Raymond stood by the bed, his arms crossed, ready to listen. As Gina and security arrived, Raymond remained in control, though visibly agitated. Fred and his colleagues maintained a safe distance.

"I'm not a bad person, he's been good to..." Sarah began.

"Are you still defending this good-for-nothing?" Raymond interrupted.

Raymond's grip on Fred tightened, but Charles and the security guard intervened, struggling to halt the clash. However, Raymond was determined to teach Fred a lesson.

"Raymond...!!"

Sarah's attempt to intervene ended with her falling from the bed.

"Sarah!!" Charles and Gina exclaimed and rushed to her on the floor.

They acted in unison to lift her from the floor and place her back on the bed. The sudden halt of the brawl brought silence to the room. All eyes were on Sarah, whose tears flowed freely.

"Sarah, are you alright? Gina, aren't you going to attend to her?" Raymond inquired with anxiety.

"What's happening, Sarah? Nurse, I think she's injured," Fred said.

Raymond's displeasure was evident in his reaction to Fred's concern. Gina's hands trembled as she watched the scene unfold.

"Let me call the doctor," Gina suggested.

"No! Don't call the doctor. I need to put an end to this now," Sarah sobbed.

"What do you mean?" Raymond and Fred chorused.

Sarah's sobs grew uncontrollable before she finally managed to speak.

"I'm deeply sorry for the animosity I've stirred between both of you. I might as well be the devil of my own success. I've always listened to others' stories, learning never to be a victim. Yet, I've made my own versions of their mistakes. I chased after dead-end opportunities while surrounded by better choices. I thought working in the mines was all I needed. I ignored Raymond's advice about my decision, assuming he wanted to control me and take advantage of my circumstances. Fred came into the picture, and despite his inability to provide the life Raymond offered, I was still determined to work in the mines. I was willing to go the extra mile to secure a position there after he helped me get into the National Service. That's where my story ends" Sarah struggled to pull back her tears.

"Two weeks ago, the doctor confirmed that my accident had left me paralyzed from the waist down. For a while, I've been pretending, acting like I was struggling. I didn't know how to tell any of you that I can no longer feel my legs. I couldn't bear to witness both of you fighting" she bowed down her head in pitty.

"What...???"

The room filled with shock as everyone voiced their disbelief in unison.

"Gina, Charles, did you know about this?" Raymond questioned, his anger simmering.

Fred and his friends were stunned, unable to process the revelation. Raymond's presence held them all captive, preventing any response that could further agitate him.

"Please, don't blame Gina or Charles. My conscience told me you would all turn your backs on me if I revealed the truth. Perhaps you've shown more care now that I'm disabled, and I tried to take advantage of that. Together with Charles and Gina, I persuaded the doctors not to discharge me when I had nowhere else to go. Besides, in my current state, I can't leave the hospital and search for a job," Sarah narrated.

Raymond's tears could no longer be contained. He knelt before her, crying uncontrollably.

"Sarah, there's something I've been wanting to ask you," Charles finally found his voice.

"Who were you meeting on that fateful day when I picked you up?" the room was abruptly silenced showing everyone's interest in the question asked by Charles.

"I regret the day I agreed to meet him. The person who caused me this harm is in this room. He must be pleased with his accomplishment now," Sarah started.

A tense atmosphere settled in as they exchanged shocked glances.

"I was at work when he called, asking to meet up to discuss some matters related to my continued employment in the mines. Filled with enthusiasm, I grabbed my bag and headed to the address he provided." At this time, the tears flowed uncontrollably down her cheeks.

"And that's how I ended up here. I've squandered all the efforts I put into my national service period. I'm certain some of my colleagues are now retained, while others are moving forward in life as long as their legs can carry them," she lamented.

"It's him...!" She sobbed.

Sarah pointed her finger at one of Fred's colleagues, her voice quivering. Enraged, Fred turned and slapped the colleague, prompting another to strike his cheek immediately. Everyone was left in shock by the unexpected turn of events. Charles swiftly called the police for the apprehension of the suspect.

The man in question was a junior worker who had been saved from layoffs by a manager and had manipulated Sarah, pretending to offer her an opportunity. His true intention was to exploit her and also gather information about Fred that could get him fired.

Sooner than expected, the police arrived. The blaring siren of a police car captured the attention of patients, visitors, and hospital staff. Sarah's ordeal had already made headlines after Fred and his colleagues sought her out on the radio. Those who witnessed the suspect being led away by the police couldn't help but condemn him for his cruel act.

"Sarah, I'm deeply sorry for all you've endured because of that monster" Fred knelt beside Sarah's bed and pleaded.

"I promise he'll face the consequences of his actions" Fred turned to face Raymond without looking into his eyes.

"Raymond... I'm... I'm... I'm truly sorry for the harm I've caused you as well. Please find it in your heart to forgive me. I convinced Sarah to leave your house for mine, but I let her down in the end. Please forgive me," Fred pleaded again with genuine remorse.

Raymond let out a heavy sigh after coming out from the deep dumbfoundedness.

"I forgive you, Fred" Raymond empathised.

"Sarah is an incredible person, and anyone would be lucky to have her. The harm has already been done, and we can't change the past. Instead, let's learn from it and move forward" he also turned to look Sarah in the eye and spoke with pity,…

"Sarah, I hold no grudge against you for what happened. I don't hold anything against Charles or Gina either. Everything happens for a reason.

I accept you as you are now, and my love for you remains unwavering. I'm ready to work together to overcome this challenge, even if it means seeking specialized medical care abroad. I'm willing to stand by you as my partner," Raymond comforted Sarah after the shocking revelation.

He stood up and embraced Sarah tightly, placing a gentle kiss on her forehead. Gina and Charles shared a hug, congratulating each other for their roles in this journey.

"I have a request," Fred interjected amidst the emotional scene.

"Go ahead," Raymond allowed.

"I want to be the best man at this wonderful wedding," Fred announced.

Laughter and embraces filled the room afterwards.

"Looks like we have another participant," Fred's colleague remarked.

Rita had been standing at the door, having overheard Raymond's voice as she was leaving the hospital. Her eyes were swollen from crying. Hearing that Raymond was getting married, she burst into tears again and fled. None could understand the scene until Raymond shared his past with them.

"I believe Gina should also be the maid of honor, and I'll be the driver, as usual," Charles chimed in.

Laughter erupted once more.

"Boss, don't forget you wanted to discuss something with me. Can you sprinkle some of this joy on me?" Charles reminded playfully.

"Oh, right, Charles. I had plans to offer you a position in my company as a token of appreciation for your support for Sarah and me. But I need to investigate further to ensure you're the right fit. Today has shown that you're capable of anything. If I find any wrongdoing, you won't like the outcome," Raymond warned, lightening the mood.

Sarah and Gina exchanged amused glances.

Phone rings...

Speaker: Hi, Raymond. This is the secretary of the investment company. I'm pleased to inform you that we've arranged a trip to Dubai for you and a guest as a gesture of appreciation for your contributions. Please find all the details in your email. We hope to receive a positive response from you.

Raymond: Wow... Thank you so much. I accept with gratitude.

Raymond's face lit up with a smile. Overwhelmed by joy, he shared the good news with everyone.

"Boss, this couldn't have come at a better time. This is actually race against time. Get married and send your wife to Dubai for the honeymoon," Charles suggested playfully.

Laughter filled the room once more.

Charles on his way home passed by Daavi's kitchen and greeted.

"When will Raymond settle his debts? If he doesn't do so by the end of the week, I'll pay him a visit at his office. This is unusual behavior for him," Daavi speculated.

Charles had always been resourceful, but this time, he found himself cornered with two looming threats. Agnes was unrelenting in her pursuit of revenge, and Daavi was set on exposing his debt to Raymond. It looked as though his chance of breakthrough was about to be destroyed.

Agnes had been dismissed from the pharmacy due to her involvement with Charles. She was determined to seek revenge against him by any means necessary. Her reputation was tarnished, and she was unwilling to let go of this wound without vengeance. She was prepared to go to great lengths, even if it meant risking her life by reporting to the police.

The police reached out to Fred and Raymond, informing them of the arrest of the culprit who knocked down Sarah. He was a young man who at that time had just learnt how to drive and was working with his father's car. On the said day, he confessed to being frustrated due to low patronage and seeing Sarah then, thought she was looking for a cab and so drove on top speed and unfortunately caused the accident. He fled the scene, assuming no one had witnessed the act because he was scared of the incurring cost and also getting arrested.

13

Life's path is a mosaic of triumphs and tribulations, but with each strand of fortitude, empathy, and insight, we craft a resilient identity, where wounds become wisdom, failures become guides, and decisions sculpt our fate.

As some characters' stories took a positive turn, others faced challenges. Sarah and Raymond embarked on a new chapter of love and happiness, while Issabella and her family found joy in their newfound peace. In contrast, Charles unwittingly opened a chapter of trouble for himself. Each character had their own wounds to heal, but some scars would serve as enduring lessons.

Life is a journey with its ups and downs. The struggles we face may take us to unexpected places, but it's important to heal for our own survival and growth. In the tapestry of life, the threads of destiny often intertwine in unexpected and profound ways, weaving a story that is uniquely our own. This tale serves as a poignant reminder that life's journey is a complex blend of joy and sorrow, triumph, and tribulation, and above all, the resilience of the human spirit.

Throughout the narrative, we've followed the lives of various characters as they navigated the tumultuous seas of their personal challenges. Sarah, once burdened by the weight of a devastating accident, found solace in Raymond's unwavering support and unconditional love. Their journey exemplified the healing power of connection and the beauty of finding strength within one another.

Fred's actions, though misguided, ultimately led to a turning point where truth and redemption intersected. His remorse and desire to make amends highlighted the capacity for change, even in the face of grave mistakes. Issabella's life exemplified the power of unmerited favor, which arises from our positive attitude and dedication to our work. Consistently striving for excellence, even when no one is watching, cultivates a reputation of integrity and earns us goodwill. This ultimately leads to rewarding outcomes when the time is right. The bonds of friendship between Charles, Gina, and their circle reflected the importance of solidarity and mutual support during life's most trying moments.

Mr. Ameyaw served as a significant influence in Raymond's life, offering a reflection of the consequences of his choices. This highlights the importance of valuing the wisdom of the elderly and learning from their experiences. Rather than dismissing their advice, we should embrace their insightful sayings and use their mistakes as a valuable guide for our own growth and development.

The narrative also shed light on the darker aspects of human nature. Agnes, driven by resentment and vengeance, represented the consequences of unchecked negative emotions. Her pursuit of revenge served as a cautionary tale, reminding us that healing and forgiveness are essential for our own well-being. Rita's story serves as a stark reminder of the consequences of misguided decisions. Her choices led to a tragic outcome, highlighting the importance of careful consideration and foresight when making choices. It teaches us to look beyond immediate gains and consider the long-term implications of our decisions, rather than focusing solely on short-term benefits.

As each character's journey unfolded, the story unveiled the profound lessons embedded within their experiences. It underscored the significance of second chances, the transformative power of compassion, and the resilience that blooms from within. The characters' growth mirrored the evolution of life itself – a dynamic blend of highs and lows that shape us into the individuals we become.

In the final moments of our journey, as the relentless clock ticked away, we found ourselves racing not only against time but also against our own limitations. We discovered that in the face of adversity, we could summon extraordinary strength, resilience, and determination. Our pursuit of the elusive victory was a testament to the indomitable human spirit, a reminder that we can achieve the impossible when the seconds slip through our fingers like grains of sand.

As we crossed the finish line, we did so not as individuals but as a family, friends, and community, forever connected by the memories we created during our exhilarating journey. In the end, we realized that the most important victory was not the one we achieved against time, but the one we achieved within ourselves and with each other. Every scar we bear, both visible and hidden, contributes to our unique tapestry. As we journey onward, may we carry the lessons of these characters in our hearts, embracing the healing power of connection, the strength that arises from embracing our vulnerabilities, and the enduring hope that brighter days await, even after the darkest of nights.

THE END!